From the Start

THE RAIDER BROTHERS

D. E. Haggerty

Copyright © 2025 D.E. Haggerty

All rights reserved.

D.E. Haggerty asserts the moral right to be identified as the author of this work.

ISBN: **9789083465579**

From the Start is a work of fiction. The names, characters, places, and incidents portrayed in it are the product of the author's imagination. Any resemblance to actual persons, living or dead, events or locations is entirely coincidental.

All rights reserved. No part of this publication may be reproduced, stored in a retrieval system, or transmitted, in any form or by any means, electronic, mechanical, photocopying, recording or otherwise, without the prior permission of the author.

No portion of this book may be reproduced in any form without written permission from the publisher or author, except as permitted by U.S. copyright law.

Also by D.E. Haggerty

Until It Was Real
For the Promise
Before It Was Love
After The Vows
While We Waited
All Along
Beyond the Hate
How to Date a Rockstar
How to Love a Rockstar
How to Fall For a Rockstar
How to Be a Rockstar's Girlfriend
How to Catch a Rockstar
My Forever Love
Forever For You
Just For Forever
Stay For Forever
Only Forever
Meet Disaster
Meet Not
Meet Dare

Meet Hate
Bragg's Truth
Bragg's Love
Perfect Bragg
Bragg's Match
Bragg's Christmas
A Hero for Hailey
A Protector for Phoebe
A Soldier for Suzie
A Fox for Faith
A Christmas for Chrissie
A Valentine for Valerie
A Love for Lexi
About Face
At Arm's Length
Hands Off
Knee Deep
Molly's Misadventures

Chapter 1

Harper – a woman with a thousand problems but no time to worry about any of them

HARPER

The lights flicker before the bar goes dark. My stomach drops to the floor, and my hands shake as I grasp the pint glass to pour a beer. I've been tapping beer since I was old enough to stand behind the bar. I can do this in the dark. No problem.

You know what is a problem? The electricity bill I may have forgotten to pay.

I've been fooling around with which bill to pay when and stretching the due dates to the extreme. I don't have much choice. Money is tight, which is an understatement to put it lightly. There never seems to be enough cash to go around.

The lights come back on, and I blow out a breath in relief. The electricity company is not cutting me off. I must have paid the bill on time after all.

I set the beer down on the bar in front of one of our regulars, Dick.

"Did you forget to pay your electricity bill, Harper?"

"Nope. I'm testing your night vision."

He chuckles as he lifts his beer.

"Get off me! Get off me!"

I sigh. Why did I want to own a bar again? Oh, yeah, I thought it would provide financial security for me and Dad. Ha! Silly me.

I hurry across the room to the man who's shouting. My brow wrinkles when I arrive at his table to discover he's alone.

"Hi. I'm Harper. I own this bar. And you are?"

"I'm Devin."

"Nice to meet you, Devin. What seems to be the problem?"

He points to the floor. "This beast won't leave me alone."

I kneel down and peek under the table to find a dog peering back at me. "Sloane!"

My bartender comes running. "There you are, Boozer." She picks up the dog and cuddles him.

"Your dog!" Devin shakes his finger at Sloane. "Assaulted me when the lights were out."

"Assaulted you? Boozer wouldn't hurt a fly." Sloane kisses the dog's nose. "Would you, boy?"

"Boy? It's a boy?"

Sloane glares at Devin. "Boozer isn't an it."

"*It* licked my face and humped my leg."

I groan. This happens every time Sloane brings her dog to the bar. Boozer is leg-humping-happy. Which is why I banned her from bringing him any more. But does she listen?

"Your next round is on me."

Devin grins at me before standing and sauntering to the bar. Probably to pick out the most expensive whiskey I stock.

"You." I point to Sloane. "Follow me."

I march to my office and usher her inside before slamming the door shut behind us.

"I told you not to bring Boozer to the bar anymore."

"But look at his face," she pouts. "Who can resist this face?"

She squashes his face with her hands and bats her eyelashes at me. I cross my arms over my chest and give her the 'look'. My employees have nicknamed it my Siren's Scowl. They think I don't know. Ha! I know everything happening in my bar.

"Sloane," I grumble. "This is a business. I can't have patrons being licked by your dog. It's not professional."

She rolls her eyes. "Did you forget *Rumrunner* is a speakeasy on a touristy island?"

I frown. I don't deny the island of Smuggler's Hideaway is touristy. It's impossible to miss with all the festivals and beach seekers, but I grew up on this island. It's my home. I don't enjoy people making negative comments about my home.

"Tourism isn't an excuse to be unprofessional."

She groans. "Are you going to give me one of your lectures about professionalism again?"

"No. What I am going to do is make you pay for whatever drink Devin wants."

Her nose wrinkles. "Who's Devin?"

"The man your dog just felt up!"

"Oh. Him."

I check the time. "You can have your break now. Take Boozer home."

"But then he'll be all alone."

I grit my teeth before I end up shouting. I promise I don't have an anger management problem. What I have is a problem with employees who don't listen to me.

"He gets sad when he's alone."

"If you don't want him to be alone, you can have the day off." I'll end up working late again, but I'm used to it.

"I need the money."

"Then, you know what you need to do."

"You're mean." She huffs before spinning around and marching out of my office.

I'm mean because I insist my employees don't bring an animal to work? Whatever. I don't have time to worry about what my workers think of me.

I quickly make a note to add the price of whatever drink Devin orders to her paycheck before returning to the bar.

"Boss!" Trent, the bouncer, shouts from across the room.

I make my way to the door. "What's up?"

"A couple of guests who don't know the password."

My brow wrinkles. "How did they get the location of *Rumrunner* if they don't know the password?"

The *Rumrunner*'s location is kept secret. You can hardly be a speakeasy if everyone knows your location. The bar is down a dark and dreary alley and there's no signage. There's merely a locked door with a small window in it.

Trent motions to a table of women sitting at a booth. "They've been texting and giggling while staring at the door. And the men outside say their women are inside."

I notice the women are wearing seashell bras.

"I hate Mermaid Karaoke season," I grumble. Mermaid Karaoke takes place at *Bootlegger* – another popular bar on the island – but it's not unusual for the mermaids and smugglers to continue their parties at my bar.

I open the speakeasy window. A group of men crowd toward the door.

"Are you going to let us in? We've been waiting forever."

"We demand to speak to the management."

"I'm the owner."

"Finally." He acts as if he's been waiting years instead of five minutes.

"You need the password to enter," I explain.

"We're here now. Do we really need a password?"

"No password. No entry."

It's not a difficult concept to comprehend, but somehow, there are always people who think an exception will be made for them. The only exception is for locals. Because they'd find a way to enter with or without the password. Smuggler's Hideaway residents are the definition of sneaky.

"How do we get the password?"

"You have to answer a riddle."

He grins. "No problem. What's the riddle?"

"I dwell where land and sea embrace. With songs that echo in moonlit space. Though I'm no fish, I have a tail. In the ocean's depths, I weave my tale. Who am I?"

"Duh. You're a fish."

Another man elbows him. "She literally said she's no fish."

"Seal."

"Not a seal," I say.

"Octopus."

I shake my head. We're going to be here all night at this rate. It's not a difficult riddle. I purposely make them easy enough to answer. I don't want to turn potential customers away. I'm operating a business here after all.

"Seagull!"

"Pearl!"

"Dolphin!"

"Coral!"

I sigh. "Do you want me to repeat the riddle, or do you prefer to shout creatures of the sea all night long?"

"Repeat it. We've got this."

"I dwell where land and sea embrace. With songs that echo in moonlit space. Though I'm no fish, I have a tail. In the ocean's depths, I weave my tale. Who am I?"

This time, the men huddle together as they try to figure out the riddle.

"Siren."

"You're getting closer."

"Sea nymph."

"Less close, but you're on the right track."

"Mermaid!"

"Ding. Ding. Ding." I open the door and usher them inside. They immediately hurry to the table of women.

"Sorry, boss," Trent says when they're out of hearing range. "I could have handled them, but they asked to speak to the management."

I brush my sweaty bangs off my forehead. "No worries."

"Harper!" my other bartender, Dave, yells. "The Depth Charge Stout keg is out, but I can't leave the bar because Sloane is on break."

"I got it."

I shoulder my way through the crowd to the wall behind the bar. I tap on the wall and a door opens to reveal the hidden walk-in cooler. People murmur behind me in awe. I smile to myself. I love this old bar with all its quirks and secrets.

My phone vibrates in my back pocket. I swipe to answer before setting my phone on a shelf while I disconnect the empty keg.

"Hey, Dad," I greet. "What's the emergency?"

I'm not exaggerating. If Dad phones, it's an emergency. There's a reason I'm the money earner for the family after all.

Welcome to my glamorous life.

Chapter 2

Kai – a goofball who might understand the meaning of the word responsibility but chooses to ignore it

KAI

I whistle as I open the door to *Buccaneer's Whiskey & Distillery*, the business I own with my five brothers. Technically, my oldest brother, Eli, owns fifty percent and the rest of us share the remaining fifty, but it's all good. I don't need the responsibility of owning a business.

"You're late," Jaxon says when I enter the distillery.

"Dude." I shake my head. "Time is a construct designed to bring the man down."

He glares at me. "We're expanding the distillery. There's a lot of work to do. As the operations manager, you need to handle this."

Ugh. I never asked to be the operations manager. Especially after I realized the operations manager is a tough job. The list of items on my to-do list is never-ending – manage the equipment to ensure safety and environmental regulations are met, manage the staff working in the production area, ensure production targets are met, coordinate movement of raw materials and finished products, etc., etc., etc.

I'm exhausted merely thinking about it all.

"I thought you'd be more laid back since you got married to Blossom."

Their marriage began as a ruse to convince Blossom's ex to stop trying to steal from her but they fell in love and now they're blissfully happy. My stomach sours. I want what they have.

But the woman I want, doesn't want me. Harper thinks I'm a child. So, she's eight years older than me. Big deal.

"I want to work less," Jaxon says. "I can't keep doing your job and mine."

I frown. "You don't do my job."

He lifts an eyebrow. "Really? Who handled the safety inspection last month?"

I bristle. "I was here."

"You were physically here, but you didn't finish the preparations we agreed upon. I did them."

This discussion could go on for hours. "I'll do better next time."

"You're only saying you'll do better to get me to shut up."

Well, yeah. Because Jaxon can go on and on about responsibility and all the other nerdy stuff. Sometimes I wonder if he's really a Raider. He hasn't got a fun bone in his body. Except he does have the Raider blue eyes. All six Raider brothers do.

I glance at my wrist. "Shouldn't we be working now?"

"You're not even wearing a watch."

"Maybe it's invisible. You know all about being invisible." I wink.

Jaxon pretended to be invisible when he was avoiding Blossom. Why he was avoiding a woman who was chasing him is beyond me. It's not as if he has tons of options as the king of nerds.

I wave as I saunter to my office down the hall from Jaxon's. When I open the door, I hear a click before glitter and confetti rain down on me.

"Gotcha!" Zane and Miles, two more Raider brothers, pop up from behind my desk.

Jaxon chuckles from behind me and I whirl around to face him. "Did you delay me to give them time to set this up?"

He shrugs. "Finish the preparations for the inspection next time."

What? My boring brother doesn't usually participate in pranks. My jaw drops to the floor and I sputter when I get a mouthful of glitter.

"We are winning the prank war!" Miles shouts and Zane high-fives him.

There's always a prank war going on between the Raider brothers. Usually, I'm in the thick of it with Miles and Zane. But recently I've been off my game.

I shake my head. "A prank doesn't count unless five out of six Raider brothers witness it."

Zane shrugs. "We can't help it if we notified Eli and Rhett but they didn't show up."

Miles narrows his eyes. "This five out of six rule isn't fair. Especially when the boring brothers don't show up the way they should."

"The way they should?" I ask. "It's the middle of a work day. We're supposed to be working."

Zane rushes to me. "I'll check his temperature while you message Dr. Allens and tell her we're bringing Kai into the emergency room."

"Got it." Miles pulls out his phone.

Zane reaches for me but I bat his hands away. "I'm not sick. I don't need a doctor."

"Are you sure?" Zane asks. "You literally said 'we're supposed to be working'."

"Words I never thought little Kai would utter," Miles adds.

I growl at the term 'little Kai'. I hate being the youngest brother. Everyone treats me like a child. I'm twenty-four. I'm a man. They should treat me as such.

"Uh oh. Is little Kai getting annoyed?" Zane pats my shoulder and I shackle his wrist.

"Don't make me break your wrist."

"Fight! Fight! Fight!" Miles shouts.

"Are you seriously fighting in the distillery?" Rhett asks as he enters my office. "Jaxon is going to kill all of you."

"He started it!" Miles and I shout at the same time.

"Jinx," I say before Miles can. He sticks his tongue out at me.

"Is this why you texted 911 to me?" Rhett fists his hands at his hips. "I don't have time for your childish behavior."

"What's wrong? Did we interrupt your private time with Dakota?" Zane wiggles his eyebrows.

Dakota is Rhett's girlfriend. She's also Eli's personal assistant and works at the distillery. Which means I had a front row seat to their courtship.

It was hilarious. Dakota wouldn't give our stuck-up brother the time of day at first. Rhett did not handle rejection very well.

I indicate Rhett's shirt. "The buttons on his shirt are uneven."

"Fuck," he mutters as he fixes his shirt.

"I thought we weren't supposed to have sex in the office anymore," Miles says.

Rhett points at Miles and Zane. "You two are not allowed to bring women in for 'private' tours of the distillery that end up with the cleaning crew complaining about finding bras and panties in the refrigerator."

"What about Kai?" Miles asks. "You didn't point at him."

I lift my hands in the air. "Because I know better than to piss Andy and Waylon off." Andy and Waylon are the distillery workers.

Zane snorts. "Liar. You don't give a shit about pissing off Andy and Waylon. You haven't brought any women back to the distillery since you laid eyes on Harper."

"Just because I'm not a player the way you and Miles are doesn't mean I haven't had any female company."

I'm lying. I haven't been with a woman since I met Harper. Or re-met Harper, I should say. I grew up on the island. I've known her since I was seventeen and trying to sneak into *Rumrunner* – the bar she owns.

But it wasn't until recently that I saw her for the first time. Really saw her.

She's strong and beautiful. I want her in my bed and in my life. But she won't give me the time of day. I'll change her mind. I'll deal with a ton of shit from my brothers in the meantime, but I will change her mind eventually.

"Harper and Kai sitting in a tree. K—"

I slap a hand over Zane's mouth before he can continue. "Don't be childish."

He pries my hand away. "Me? I'm the one who's childish? You're the baby, or have you forgotten?"

I roll my eyes. "You're one year older than me. Big deal."

"It is a big deal. I…"

He trails off when Dakota barges into the room. "What's the emergency? Is everything okay? Who do I need to call? Fire department? Police department? Electricity company?"

Rhett tags her hand and draws her near. He kisses her forehead. "There's no emergency."

She scowls. "Then why did they…" She scans the room and notices the glitter and confetti. "Oh. The prank war continues."

"You should go home for lunch if you don't want to get interrupted," Miles says.

She snorts. "Right. Home. Where we'll have two small children and a dog to interrupt us. Great plan."

"How are Mira and Pearl doing?" I ask. "Am I still their favorite uncle?"

Pearl and Mira are the two children Rhett and Dakota are currently fostering. Dakota doesn't want to have her own children due to some health issues, but she's always wanted to be a foster parent. Although, I doubt Mira and Pearl will ever leave their care.

"I don't know." Dakota taps her chin and I notice a gleam in her eye. "But I bet if you babysit them this weekend, you will be."

I groan. "You want me to babysit so the two of you can have date night."

"Duh." She rolls her eyes. "What's the sense in having five uncles if they don't babysit?"

"Fine."

"And this time," Rhett grumbles. "You won't get into the paint. We spent two hours bathing the girls after the previous time you babysat."

I hold up my hands. "It wasn't my fault. Pearl conned me."

Dakota narrows her eyes at me. "My five-year-old daughter conned you?"

"She's a genius. She convinced me you said it was okay."

She shakes her finger at me. "No paint and no glitter."

"What about confetti?"

"Don't make me phone Harper and tell her you wet the bed until you were ten."

"I did not wet the bed until I was ten. You're devious."

She smirks. "You have to be devious to fit in with this family."

Rhett kisses her cheek. "You fit in with this family just fine."

Miles grins at her. "I approve of this devious side."

She points to the door. "Good. Because if you don't get back to your office and answer the phone – it's been ringing off the hook all morning – I'm going to hide all of your surfboards."

Miles loves his surfboards more than he loves this family. He planned to become a professional surfer, but a rotator cuff injury during a competition in Hawaii ruined those dreams.

"I never wanted a sister anyway," he mutters as he marches away.

When Dakota aims her gaze at Zane, he rushes for the door. "On my way to my office."

"No more pranks in the distillery," she shouts after him. "Jaxon will get mad, and he'll complain to Blossom, and I'll never hear the end of it. But I can't complain. Apparently, I have to allow my best friend to vent as often as she wants.'

"Jaxon approved this prank," I tell her.

She widens her eyes. "What did you do?"

I open my mouth to answer but she holds up her hand before I can speak. "Never mind. I'll find out from Blossom."

Rhett nods to the confetti and glitter. "Get this cleaned up."

"Why do I have to clean it up? It's not my mess."

He doesn't answer. He waves as he leads Dakota out of my office and down the hallway.

Typical. The youngest always gets stuck with the chores no one else wants to do. As I clean my office, I plot my next prank.

If Zane and Miles think they can win the prank war, they have another thing coming.

Chapter 3

"I just needed a box of Fruit Loops." ~ Harper

HARPER

I groan as I pull into the grocery store parking lot. It's packed. I shouldn't have waited until Saturday afternoon to do my groceries, but it's the first opportunity I've had all week.

And I can't wait any longer. Dad nearly lost his mind when there was no Fruit Loops cereal for breakfast this morning. A grown man shouldn't be eating Fruit Loops but you try arguing with my dad about it. I've given up.

I manage to squeeze my car into a spot at the rear of the parking lot. It may technically be a spot for a motorcycle but if the car fits, does it matter?

I open the door and am immediately assaulted with loud music. This is Smuggler's Hideaway. There's always some festival or celebration happening. But it usually isn't this loud. And there usually aren't screaming women.

What is going on? Did Hudson Clark – former NFL wide receiver and local hero – venture into town without a t-shirt again? The last time he went jogging without a shirt on, the police had to get involved. Hudson's wife, Nova, was not amused.

I force my way through the crowd toward the entrance of the grocery store.

"Hey!" a woman shouts. "You can't budge the line."

"Budge the line?" Is everyone waiting to enter the grocery store? If this is the line, Dad can forget about his Fruit Loops.

"Don't act all innocent." A woman elbows me. It's a good thing I'm used to dealing with rowdy crowds or I'd be on the ground crying in pain.

I hold up my palms. "I just need to buy some Fruit Loops. And some milk. And maybe a loaf of bread."

"I don't care what you need to buy. You're not getting in line in front of me."

I scan the area for some clue as to what in the world is going on, but it's impossible to see beyond the crowd jostling me. I glance toward the sky – hoping for some help from above – and swear under my breath when I notice the sign.

Warning: Contents May Be Too Hot. Meet the Contestants Competing for Smuggler's Sexiest Man.

One of the many, many initiatives the mayor of Smuggler's Rest – one of the three villages on Smuggler's Hideaway – established to bring in tourists was the sexiest man on the island competition. The contest came under fire last year as one of the requirements to vote for a man is that you have to kiss him. But the mayor, Lana, dropped the kiss rule and continued the contest.

I don't have time for this. Dad will have to suffer through breakfast tomorrow without his beloved Fruit Loops. I whirl around to march back to my car but then I realize – coffee. I don't have any coffee in the house.

I can put up with a lot – men flirting with me at the bar, getting beer poured all over me, women shouting at me for kicking them out of the bar – but I can't live without coffee. It's inhumane.

I reverse direction and force my way through the crowd toward the entrance of the grocery store once again. Women try to stop me by tripping me, elbowing me, and shoving me, but I keep going. I'm not playing their sexiest man games today.

But then a woman grabs hold of my ponytail and yanks. Oh no, she didn't.

I drop to my knees – forcing her to release her hold – before spinning around to confront her.

She sneers at me. "You're going down, bitch."

"Bring it on."

We begin to circle each other. The crowd notices and cheers break out. "Fight! Fight! Fight!"

Great. Not only am I not going to get Dad's Fruit Loops or my coffee. At this rate, I'm going to be late to work. Someone needs to start a grocery delivery service on the island because I don't have time for this.

But I don't back down. I never do.

"Harper!" a man shouts.

I glance over my shoulder, where I notice a stage and walkway are set up. There's a lineup of men strutting across the stage. They're all shirtless and wearing kerchiefs to cover the lower half of their faces.

"Harper!" the man shouts again as he jumps off the stage.

My breath nearly catches at the acrobatic move and how his abs contract as he lands. He prowls toward me and I can't help myself from staring at the muscles on his chest and arms. I didn't think men with this type of muscle definition existed outside of the romance novels I love to read when no one's looking.

"Harper," he grumbles, "are you okay?"

I force my gaze away from his chest to his face. Blue eyes greet me. Deep blue eyes, the color of the ocean on a hot summer day. Blue eyes I'd recognize anywhere.

Oh, dear mermaid. I've been drooling over Kai. The man-child.

"Harper." He reaches for my hand, but I retreat a step. Straight into the fist of the woman. She connects with my jaw and I go down.

Except I don't land on the ground. Kai catches me.

"Shit, Harper. Are you okay?"

I try to form words, but the feel of Kai's arms around me has my body short-circuiting. He lifts me into the air.

"Move out of my way," he demands and the crowd parts for him.

I shiver at the command in his voice. I've never heard Kai be anything but light-hearted and goofy. His deep voice commanding a crowd has my nipples pebbling.

Whoa! Nipples pebbling. The hit to my jaw must be worse than I thought. I must be concussed. No way does my body get all revved up for a male who's eight years younger than me. He's practically a child!

Kai carries me to the Red Cross Station behind the stage. Say what you will about how crazy Smuggler's Hideaway can get, but we always prioritize safety. Thus, a Red Cross Station at an event to showcase men vying to be crowned the sexiest man on the island.

He sets me down on a chair. As soon as he releases me, I feel cold and abandoned. Abandoned? What is wrong with me? Am I so desperate for male companionship that I'm lusting after a child?

"I need help here!" Kai yells.

Yep. I'm desperate for male companionship. There's no other explanation for the explosion of butterflies in my stomach at the sound of a man's growly voice.

A paramedic rushes to me but I wave him away.

"I'm fine." Revved up hormones is not a medical emergency. Not even on Smuggler's Hideaway.

"She was hit on the jaw and is dazed."

I glare at Kai. "I'm not dazed from a simple hit on the jaw. I could have taken her."

"Sure, you could, Slugger."

I narrow my eyes at him. "Do not patronize me."

He lifts his hands. "Me? Patronize you? I thought I didn't understand the meaning of the word."

I frown. Did I tell him he didn't understand the meaning of patronize? It's possible. Kai Raider has been a thorn in my side for months now with his blatant sexual innuendos and numerous requests for a date.

"I'll …" The paramedic backs away and leaves us alone.

"I'm sorry if I offended you," I begin, "but you can't blame me for getting frustrated."

"Frustrated?"

I glare at him. "Do not act all innocent with me. You hit on me several times a night every time you come to *Rumrunner*."

"I'm persistent."

"I think you mean pest."

He tugs his bandana away from his face and scowls. "Do you seriously think I'm a pest?"

Crap. He sounds hurt. I don't want to hurt him. Despite what my employees and the patrons of the bar think, I'm not a cruel person.

"I just needed a box of Fruit Loops. How was I supposed to know there was a male stripper show happening in the parking lot of the grocery store?"

"We weren't stripping."

I raise an eyebrow.

"Yet."

Great. The crowd will go wild once the men begin removing their clothes. I probably should get to work and prepare for a busy night. No coffee for me. I can always beg Parker from *Pirate's Pastries* to deliver to my house. She's done it before.

I stand. "I need to get to work."

"The paramedic hasn't checked you out yet."

"I'm fine." I alternate touching my nose with my finger. "Completely steady."

He frowns. "I don't like this."

"Too bad. You don't get a say."

He grasps my hand. I nearly jump from the jolt of electricity I feel at his touch.

"You feel it, too," he whispers and shuffles closer.

I yank my hand away. "Doesn't matter what I feel. You're immature and childish and way too young for me."

"You're never going to give me a chance, are you?"

The hurt in his blue eyes slays me. I don't want to hurt him. I never want to hurt anyone. But I seem to accidentally hurt people all the time. It's my special skill.

"I'm sorry, Kai. But no."

Our gazes meet for a long moment. I want to erase the words I spoke. But I can't. My life is beyond busy. I'm barely managing as it is. I can't handle one more thing to look after.

And, make no mistake about it, I'd be looking after Kai if we were in a relationship. There's no way he'd look after me. And I want a man who will carry some of the burden for me. Not add to mine.

Kai flashes me a smile. "Don't worry. I'll change your mind."

I groan. Great. A persistent man-child. Exactly what I need.

"After you." He motions me forward.

"After me?"

"I'll walk you to work since you're too stubborn to get examined by a paramedic. I know all about head injuries."

I snort. "I bet you do."

Chapter 4

"Technically, he said no paint." ~ Kai

KAI

I notice the time on the clock as I park. Shit. I'm late. Rhett is going to have my ass. If Dakota doesn't get to me first. I promised I wouldn't be late to babysit their kids today.

I hurry out of my car and rush to the front door. It flies open before I reach it. Dakota taps her foot as she glares at me.

"Sorry. I'm late. I was ready early, so I decided to clean the house."

She lifts an eyebrow. "Clean the house? Is that what we're calling pranking these days?"

My nose wrinkles. "I didn't prank anyone."

She shakes her phone at me. "But you did make a Pinterest board with a ton of prank ideas."

"I thought I made my board private," I mutter.

Rhett joins us on the porch. "Good. You're on time."

"On time?"

Dakota groans. "I told him the wrong time to make sure he got here on time. But now he knows my trick."

"Uncle Kai," Pearl shouts as she darts out of the house. I lift her up in the air and she giggles.

"Who's your favorite uncle?"

"Kai! Kai! Kai!" she shouts.

I kiss her cheek as a reward and she giggles. The sound warms my heart. Pearl was shy and afraid of everyone and everything when she arrived at Rhett and Dakota's house a few months ago. But now she's a terror. I'm very proud of my influence on her.

"Are you going to be good for Uncle Kai?" Dakota asks.

Pearl bats her eyelashes. "Yes, Mom."

Tears form in Dakota's eyes. Pearl has only been calling her mom for a week. Although Pearl and her half-sister Mira are technically foster children, Rhett is doing everything he can to adopt them. Having a big brother who's a billionaire doesn't hurt.

Don't get me wrong. Eli never throws the wealth he earned as a founder of *Apparoo* around. But he also doesn't hesitate to use his influence to help his family. Such as founding a distillery so all of his brothers have jobs and can stay on Smuggler's Hideaway.

"No getting into the paint," Rhett orders.

"Yes, Dad."

My niece is good. She has Rhett and Dakota wrapped around her adorable little finger.

"Mira is in bed. She should be out for the night. She's a good little sleeper," Dakota tells me before kissing Pearl. "Be good for Uncle Kai."

Rhett hands me the baby monitor. "No paint."

"Get out of here. Pearl and I have plans that do not involve boring parents."

Dakota doesn't move from the porch. For someone who wants 'date night' with her boyfriend, she doesn't appear eager to leave.

"It'll be fine. Kai won't allow our babies to be hurt. Unless he wants to die." Rhett glares at me.

I salute him. "I will not hurt my favorite nieces."

Rhett grasps Dakota's hand and leads her to their car. I stand on the porch with Pearl and wave to them until they're out of sight.

"They're gone. What do you want to do? Go surfing, sky-diving, ride rollercoasters at *Mermaid Mystical Gardens*? Name your poison."

She giggles. "I'm too young to do any of those things."

"Young? Phew. What a relief. I thought there was a problem with your growth."

"You're silly, Uncle Kai."

"But fun, right?"

I set her down and she scampers inside. I shut the door behind me. The second the door is shut, Delphine trots toward me. I get to my knees. "Who's a good girl?"

Her tail thumps as I pet her ears. I dig a doggy treat out of my pocket and feed it to her.

"Delphine can't have treats."

I gasp. "Says who?"

"Mom and Dad."

I wrinkle my nose. "What Mom and Dad don't know won't hurt them."

She giggles. "Shall we get the paint out?"

No way. No how. It's impossible to paint with a four-year-old without her parents finding out. I have learned my lesson there. But I've been googling fun stuff to do with a small child and I have some ideas.

"Do you want to hear my idea?"

She bounces on her toes. "Yes!"

I place a finger over my mouth. "We have to be quiet. Your sister is sleeping."

"Yes," she whisper-shouts.

"We could make a mud kitchen."

Her nose wrinkles. "Dad gets mad when I eat mud."

"Okay. How about playdough?"

"Boring."

I tap my chin. "What about painting with colored sand?"

I came up with this idea because I know how much Pearl loves to paint – the girl is an artist in the making – but I don't want Rhett to shave my hair off in my sleep because I got his precious daughter dirty with paint again.

"We don't have colored sand."

I smirk. "But I do."

She claps. "Yea!"

"Shall we check on your sister before we get our supplies?" I tag Pearl's hand and we make our way down the hallway to the baby's room.

I love this room. Dakota went all out decorating it. She even hired a local artist to paint a mural on the wall. Since this is Smuggler's Hideaway, the mural is full of mermaids, smugglers, seals, and otters.

Speaking of seals and otters, there are life-sized stuffed animals of a seal and an otter on the floor. The mobile above the crib features otters, raccoons, and parrots. Rhett commissioned it since his first date with Dakota was an attempt to steal Plank, the foul-mouthed parrot.

Each town on Smuggler's Hideaway has a live mascot. Smuggler's Rest has Viking the otter. Rogue's Landing has Rogue the raccoon. And Pirate's Perch has Plank.

I tiptoe toward the crib. Mira is fast asleep on her back with her arms and legs spread out in the shape of a jellyfish. I resist the urge to kiss her cheek. I don't want to wake her.

I shut the door to the nursery behind us before leading Pearl to my car, where my supplies are. I grab a bag full of squeeze bottles filled with colored sand and we return to the kitchen.

"We need to cover the dining room table before we begin."

Pearl rushes off and returns with some papers.

"Perfect."

Once the paper is spread out on the table, I set the squeeze bottles with red, pink, purple, yellow, and blue sand on the table.

"What do I do?" Pearl asks.

"You can draw whatever you want with the sand. Here. Let me show you." I use the yellow to make a smiley face.

"I'm going to draw a princess!"

She gathers all the colors to her before starting to squirt the sand onto the paper. The princess has a purple and yellow gown and blue hair.

I play around with the red color.

"Why don't you have children?" Pearl asks as she works.

"I don't have a wife yet." I won't be the first person to explain to Pearl how it's possible to have children without being married. Rhett would throw me off the cliff at *Mermaid Mystical Gardens* if I explained the birds and the bees to his precious daughter.

"Why don't you have a wife?"

"Ah, that's a tough question." I can hardly tell my adorable little niece, the woman I want doesn't want me.

Harper. Merely thinking about her has my heartbeat speeding up and warmth spreading through my body.

Harper is beyond a doubt the most beautiful woman I've ever seen. She has shoulder-length brown hair and light blue eyes. Eyes, I'd love to watch flare with passion. When she smiles, she has a dimple on each cheek. Unfortunately, she doesn't smile around me much.

And then there are her curves. She's short but has curves in all the right places. My fingers itch to dig into her hips. And my mouth waters to taste her breasts.

But there's more to Harper than her beauty. She's wicked smart. The hardest worker I've ever met and I have three brothers who are workaholics. She's tough and grumpy, but I've glimpsed a softer side of her. A softer side I'm determined to see more of.

"Uncle Kai!" Pearl yells before squirting sand into my face.

I bat the sand away. "Why are you attacking me?"

"You weren't listening."

"I was too listening." I pick up my red bottle and squirt her top with it.

She squeals before gathering the sand on the paper and throwing it at me.

I punch my hand in the air. "This is war!"

Pearl giggles before jumping from her chair and racing away from me. I chase after her. The front door flies open and I freeze. Rhett is standing at the door, glaring at me.

"What are you doing back home?"

"Dakota forgot her purse." He points at the table. "I told you no painting."

"Technically, you said no paint."

"And you decided to use colored sand in the house?" He stalks toward the table and picks up a piece of paper. "While using the quarterly report as your background."

I cringe. "I assumed it was an old report. Who prints out reports anymore?"

Dakota walks inside. "What's taking so long?" She glances around. "Oh."

"Pearl started it."

She fists her hands on her hips. "You're blaming my five-year-old daughter for this mess?"

"Is this a trick question?"

She reaches down and picks Pearl up. "You can clean up this mess while we go for dinner."

I survey the room. There's sand all over the kitchen floor, as well as a trail of sand through the living room. I groan. I hate cleaning up. Who doesn't?

"Bring me back a doggy bag?" I bat my lashes and do my best to appear innocent.

Dakota snorts. "There's frozen pizza in the freezer."

My nose wrinkles. "What am I? A destitute college student?"

Rhett hands me the vacuum cleaner as he passes me. "Don't wake the baby."

They shut the door behind them, leaving me with the mess to clean up. At least I'm still Pearl's favorite uncle.

Chapter 5

"I don't want to see another box of Fruit Loops in my life ever again." ~ Harper

HARPER

"Where are my Fruit Loops?"

I jar awake at the shouted question.

"Harper!"

I blow out a breath and search for some patience before I scream back. Trust me. Screaming back at my dad doesn't help.

I roll out of bed, grab a sweatshirt from the floor, and stumble my way to the kitchen.

"Good morning, Dad."

He grunts in response. And everyone says I'm the grump. Ha! They obviously haven't met my father.

"What's the problem?" I ask.

"There aren't any Fruit Loops."

"I'm sorry. I didn't make it to the grocery store yesterday." My jaw aches to remind me why.

"You should let me go to the grocery store by myself."

Ugh. Not this again. Dad suffered a moderate stroke shortly after Mom died. He did rehab and has regained quite a bit of his mobility, but his right arm and leg never fully recovered. He gets around with a cane pretty well, but the grocery store is too far for him. And he refuses to use a motorized wheelchair.

"You can go to the grocery store by yourself," I begin and he smiles, "if you use a motorized wheelchair."

"I am not using a motorized wheelchair ever again."

"You can't walk to the grocery store from here. It's too far."

"Bullshit. I can do it."

I lift an eyebrow. "Did you forget what happened last time?"

His cheeks darken. "You shouldn't shame a man for having an accident."

"I'm not trying to shame you. I'm reminding you of how the police called me because you were caught relieving yourself in the neighbor's rose bushes."

"It was fertilizer."

"And then you sat down on the chair inside the other neighbor's playhouse and couldn't get back up."

"Damn chair was tiny."

"Because it was a child's playhouse."

"If your mother was here, she'd let me go to the grocery store."

His shot hits me straight in the chest where he aimed. I struggle to breathe for a second. Mom was the sweetest, kindest person to ever walk this earth. She was also a pushover for my dad. Whatever he wanted, she gave him.

I've never seen love the way my parents loved each other. It was beautiful to behold. But then my mom got sick and died when I was a freshman in high school. Dad had a stroke a year later.

According to Google, there's no way the stroke could have been caused by heartbreak. I disagree. I witnessed my vibrant, loving dad shrivel away after Mom died.

Since sophomore year of high school, I've been in charge of managing this house, making sure Dad makes it to his doctor's appointments, overseeing Dad's recovery, and paying all the bills once Dad's benefits ran out.

It's the reason I bought the *Rumrunner* when I had the chance. I didn't realize I should have hired an accountant to review the sales price. I'll be paying off the bar until the day I die.

"I'm sorry, Dad, but Mom's not here."

He glances away from me but not before I notice the pain in his eyes. It's been sixteen years – half of my life – and he's still grieving for the woman he loves.

"You're stuck with me. And I got in a fight in the grocery store parking lot and didn't manage to buy your Fruit Loops before the bar opened up yesterday."

He scowls. "Why'd you do a fool thing like get in a fight?"

"I was provoked."

"One of these days, your temper is going to get the worst of you."

I shrug. "It's not my fault the woman thought I was budging in line."

"It's never your fault."

I poke my tongue out at him. "How about I make some pancakes for breakfast?"

He perks up. "With butter and maple syrup?"

I nod. "With butter and maple syrup."

Ever since Dad's stroke, we've been on a healthy diet in this household. Plenty of fruits and vegetables, wholegrains and high fiber breads and cereals, lean meats, poultry, and fish. The one exception is Fruit Loops for breakfast.

I've tried my best to rid Dad of his Fruit Loops addiction, but there's only so much I can do when he decides to protest by refusing to go to therapy. You try carrying a grown man into a car and then we'll talk.

I gather the ingredients I need for the pancakes and switch on the griddle. The doorbell rings.

"I'll get it."

"Go ahead. It's not for me anyway."

I frown. Dad used to have an active social life when Mom was alive. Now he doesn't speak to any of his friends. His friends stopped coming around when he refused to open the door for them.

I need to do something about his social life. Dad's in his fifties. He has years of living ahead of him. He's way too young to give up on life.

"Hey," I greet Parker when I open up the door.

She lifts up a coffee and small bag. "As requested."

"You're a lifesaver."

She giggles. "True. I save lives as a pastry chef all the time."

I open the bag and inhale the scent of chocolate and cinnamon. "Total lifesaver."

"It's a Siren's Snap cookie. I put my own twist on the classic ginger snap."

"I don't know why you're still in Smuggler's Hideaway and not baking in a patisserie in Paris but I thank the mermaids every day for it."

"My French sucks anyway," she jokes but her smile is strained.

There's a story there, but I've never had the chance to dig into the past with Parker. She works early morning hours at the bakery, and I work late hours at the bar. We're two ships passing in the night.

"Are you going to leave the door open all day and let all the flies in?" Dad – my very own reason for not leaving Smuggler's Hideaway – complains.

"Do you want to come in? I'll share my cookie with you."

"You'd share a cookie with me?"

I frown. "I know how to share."

She snorts. "Which is why you got detention in second grade for refusing to share your crayons with Sophia."

"Sophia broke all of her crayons and threw them at Flynn."

She rolls her eyes. "Those two were destined for each other from a young age."

Sophia – a friend of ours who is part owner of the local brewery – was a year behind us in school, but in a place the size of Smuggler's Hideaway, everyone knows everyone. And everyone knows everything about everyone.

"I heard you got in a fight yesterday. I thought you'd have a shiner."

Told you. Everyone knows everything about everyone. But the details are often a bit fuzzy.

"I didn't get into a fight."

She lifts her eyebrows.

"It was a scuffle at most."

"And Kai Raider came to your rescue."

I scowl. "Kai Raider didn't come to my rescue."

"I heard he jumped off stage, ran to you, and picked you up and carried you to the ER when you got knocked out."

"I did not get knocked out," I growl. "And I didn't go to the ER."

"But he did jump off stage and pick you up?"

I grunt. There's only one reason why she's being this persistent. "Are you seriously betting on whether Kai and I will get together?"

She shrugs. "The man has been pursuing you hard for the past few months."

"Man? Are we still discussing Kai?"

"He's twenty-four. Legal."

"Holy smugglers. You make me sound like a cougar."

"If the claws fit."

"I do not want a younger man. I want a man who will help lighten my load, not make it heavier."

"Sorry." Her nose wrinkles. "How's your dad doing anyway?"

"I'm being assaulted by two thousand angry flies who got into the house because my daughter doesn't know how to close a door," Dad shouts from the living room where he's sitting on his favorite chair watching television.

"And there's the answer to your question."

Parker giggles. I don't find the situation amusing, but I keep my growl contained. *Pirates Pastries* is struggling. She could use a bit of laughter in her life.

"Do you want to come in? I'm making pancakes."

"Nah. I better get back to the bakery. I left Holly in charge. Her teenage friends will devour every pastry I've ever made if I don't stop them."

"Okay, but let's grab a coffee and catch up soon."

"Sounds good. I'll schedule you in for some time in 2030, which is when I assume the next time we both have time off aligns."

"I'll order an agenda for 2030."

She waves as she walks off. I shut the door behind her.

"It's about damn time. I'm starving. Where are my pancakes? Or can I have your cookie?"

Pfff... The 2030 comment wasn't far off.

Chapter 6

"Age is just a number." ~ Kai

KAI

"I expect us to win the escape room this year," Eli says.

This weekend is the *Bootlegger Escape Room* festival. Teams compete to be the fastest through a bootlegger themed escape room. Last year, we lost to the owners of the *Five Fathoms Brewery*. Although, I'm pretty sure the owners – Sophia, Chloe, Nova, Maya, and Paisley – cheated somehow.

I wiggle my eyebrows. "Afraid you'll lose to your fiancé?"

Paisley – the master brewer at *Five Fathoms* – and Eli fell in love when a hurricane destroyed the brewing facilities and the brewery temporarily brewed beer in the distillery.

I had a blast watching those two try and hide their office 'trysts' from everyone. Did they seriously think they could hide from us? As if.

Speaking of office trysts. "Where's Blossom?" I ask Jaxon.

"My wife didn't want to participate in the rivalry between the distillery and the brewery."

Makes sense. Blossom is Paisley's assistant, but she's also married to Jaxon, the master distiller of *Buccaneer's Whiskey*. Plus, she's the most competitive woman I've ever met and can't handle losing.

"She's meeting us at *Rumrunner* later," he adds.

My pulse spikes at the mention of *Rumrunner*. Harper. I can't wait to see her again. She claims she won't ever give me a chance, but I saw the way her blue eyes sparkled when I touched her. I know she felt the spark between us. It was undeniable.

"I'm surprised Harper agreed to provide the winning prize again this year," Rhett says.

I frown. The winning prize is free drinks at *Rumrunner* all night. "Why wouldn't she agree?"

Harper can be grumpy, but she's a native Smuggler. She wouldn't refuse to provide a prize for a local festival.

"She asked for a payment plan to pay for her latest delivery of whiskey."

I stare at Rhett but he doesn't crack a joke or glance away to indicate he's lying. Shit. Is Harper's business in trouble? I don't get it. *Rumrunner* is packed every time I'm there. She should be making a good living.

"Raider brothers!" Lana, the mayor of Smuggler's Rest, shouts. "You're up next!"

Eli herds us toward the starting line. "We are winning this."

"Did we win?" Miles asks an hour later as he stumbles his way down the alley toward *Rumrunner*.

Zane throws an arm around his shoulder and they nearly collapse on the ground. I rush to help them stand.

"We did win, didn't we?" Zane slurs.

Eli grunts. "We tied. I don't understand how we tied."

I lift an eyebrow. "Maybe because your 'idea' was stolen from Paisley."

Every time you complete a task during the escape room quest, you have to drink a shot of moonshine. Except there's actually no requirement for each participant to drink a shot. The rule is, the shots have to be drunk.

It's a loophole Paisley discovered. I knew they cheated last year! She made the unfortunate mistake of telling Eli about it.

When he told us about the loophole, Zane and Miles volunteered to drink all of the shots of moonshine so that Rhett, Jaxon, and Eli would be sober enough to answer the escape room questions.

Jaxon glares at Zane. "We would have won outright if you hadn't tried to answer a question."

"How was I supposed to know moonshine during Prohibition was made of corn?"

Jaxon purses his lips. "I told you the answer and you refused to listen."

"But rye is a legitimate grain for whiskey making," Zane insists.

"We weren't discussing whiskey making."

We arrive at the hidden door to the speakeasy and I knock. Trent opens the speakeasy window and scowls when he notices me keeping Miles upright.

"We're here to celebrate," Miles slurs.

The bouncer opens the door and motions us inside. "Don't cause any trouble or Harper will kick you out."

I glance toward the bar. Harper is scowling at us.

"We'll behave," I yell across the room toward her.

"Didn't know the word behave was in your vocabulary."

I shrug. "The teachers at school were always telling me to behave. Not sure what they meant."

She shakes her head but her lips tip up. I accept victory for this round.

I half-drag, half-carry Miles to our usual table. We pass the women from the brewery on the way.

"Losers!" Sophia taunts.

"If we're losers, you are as well since we tied," Jaxon says.

She shakes a finger at him. "Don't use your nerdy logic on me, whiskey boy. I'm not Blossom."

Paisley frowns. "If you had let me answer the question on the main difference between distilling spirits and brewing beer, we would have won."

Sophia's nose wrinkles. "I was certain higher temperatures for distilling was the answer."

Paisley purses her lips. "And you wonder why I insist you don't set foot in my brewery."

Miles pitches forward, but I manage to stop him before he face plants on the floor of the bar. "A little help here."

Zane rushes to help and trips over his own feet. Rhett catches him and steers him toward our table.

Harper arrives with a bottle of moonshine and six glasses.

"Moonshine!" Miles cheers and Zane high-fives him. Except he misses Miles's hand and ends up slapping his face.

"Why are you slapping me?" Miles asks as he rubs his cheek.

Harper snatches the bottle back. "Maybe moonshine isn't a good idea. Shall I bring you some coffee?"

"Coffee?" Miles feigns throwing up. "I want moonshine."

"And I don't want to clean vomit up. You can't always get what you want."

"I'll clean up any vomit," I offer.

Zane rears back. "You'll clean up vomit? You hate to clean up vomit. You're a sympa- sympa…"

"Sympathetic vomiter," Miles offers.

I shrug. "I can wear a face mask."

"Whoa. You wear a face mask?" Miles leans close to meet my gaze and nearly headbutts me. "Are you trying to flirt?"

"Flirt?" Zane attempts to snort and ends up coughing instead.

I sigh. "Maybe coffee is a good idea after all."

Miles stands. "Who is this man?" He points at me. I duck before he pokes me in my eye since his aim isn't the best at the moment. "Does anyone know who this man is?"

"Dude, if you've forgotten I'm your brother, you've had enough to drink."

"My brother? My brother?" He weaves and I pull him back down before he falls. "My brother doesn't drink coffee in a bar."

Everyone in the bar aims their gaze at me. My cheeks warm but I ignore it.

"I love coffee."

"In the morning when you deign to arrive at the office," Jaxon says.

Harper sets the bottle back on the table. "I don't have time for this. If you want coffee, you can order at the bar."

I grin at her. "Thank you for bringing the moonshine."

She narrows her eyes at me. "Why are you sober?"

Because I didn't want to be under the influence when I saw her again.

"Thanks for noticing. I knew you liked me." I wink.

She huffs. "Give it up, man-child."

"Never, Slugger."

She grunts before marching away. I keep my eyes on her ass. The woman has curves for days. Curves I want to explore with my hands and my tongue. My cock twitches. It's tired of waiting. Too bad. It's going to have to wait some more.

Harper isn't some woman you pick up at a bar for a quickie. She's a woman who needs to be wooed.

Speaking of wooing. I stand. "Excuse me."

Eli groans. "Kai."

I blink and give him my best innocent look. "What?"

"Give it up. Harper isn't interested in you."

"She wasn't complaining when I carried her the other day."

Nope. She smuggled into me and petted my abs. She's interested. But she's resisting me because she thinks I'm too young. It's the twenty-first century. Age doesn't matter anymore. It's just a number.

I saunter toward the bar, but when Harper notices me, she scurries to the storage room. Good. She'd fight me for what I'm about to do.

"I don't have time for whatever this is," Sloane says when I reach the bar.

"I'm not here to cause problems. I'm here to help."

"If you're here to help." She throws a towel at me. "Get to pouring the beer."

This is working out even better than I expected. I make my way behind the bar.

"Where's the order?"

She shows me how to bring up the orders, and I get to work.

"What are you doing?" I nearly jump at Harper's question. I manage to stop tapping the beer before it overflows and place it on the waiting tray.

"What does it look like I'm doing?"

She scowls. "I didn't hire you to work behind my bar."

"I'm merely helping out. If you don't need my help, I'll go back to my brothers." I nod toward the line waiting for service at the bar.

"I can handle this."

"I know you can. My slugger can handle anything."

She blows out a breath. "I'm not your slugger. I'm not a slugger at all. I wasn't the one handing out punches."

"Because you were too busy being distracted by my manly chest on display." I wiggle my eyebrows.

She snorts. "I was merely surprised you didn't have a chest full of tattoos you got while you were too drunk to remember."

"No tattoos. I don't let any random person touch my chest."

Her eyes flare before she clears her throat. "If you want to spend your Saturday night working for free, be my guest."

"Oh, now I'm your guest."

"I can't with you. I just can't..." She throws her arms in the air before walking off.

Sloane nudges me. "More beer pouring and less drooling over the boss, Casanova."

I get back to work but this time with a smile on my face. Harper is warming to me. I'll keep hammering at the ice around her heart until she finally melts in my arms.

All the effort will be worth it in the end. Harper's worth it.

Chapter 7

"Kai needs to look the word romantic up in the dictionary because he doesn't have a clue what it means."
~ Harper

HARPER

My phone rings and wakes me. I groan and cover my head with my pillow.

I didn't get home last night until six. I guess I should say this morning. I am not getting out of this bed for the phone.

"Answer your phone, Harper," Dad yells. "Or I'll come in there and tell whoever it is you can't answer the phone because you've been abducted by aliens and are getting probed."

I smile at the threat. Dad used to do crazy shit all the time before Mom died. One time, he had the school convinced I was having an operation to have my sixth and seventh toes removed from both my feet. Mom didn't let him answer the phone after that.

"Go away!"

He pounds his cane on the floor. "Answer your phone. The aliens are circling above us."

I giggle as I reach for my phone.

"Hello."

"Harper. Good morning. It's Jerry."

I sit up in bed. It can't be a good thing if my accountant is phoning me on a Monday morning.

"What's wrong? What bill did I forget to pay this time? Please tell me they aren't threatening to shut my water off."

He chuckles. "Your water is safe."

"Then, what's the problem?"

"I wanted to check a transaction with you from last night."

"Okay?"

"There's one transaction from last night in the amount of several thousand dollars. I want to make sure it's not a mistake."

"Several thousand dollars?" I brush the hair out of my face. "No one's bar tab was over a thousand dollars last night."

And I would know. If a bar tab reaches five hundred dollars, my system alerts me and I make the table cash out. I can't afford for patrons to not pay their big tabs.

"The name on the credit card is Kai Raider."

"Say the name again?" I must have misheard. No way did Kai pay a bar tab of several thousand dollars last night. He was supposed to drink for free since his team won the *Bootlegger Escape Room Festival.*

"The name on the card is Kai Raider."

What the hell was he thinking? "I'll deal with it, Jerry," I say before hanging up.

I scroll through my contacts but I don't have Kai's number. I drum my fingers on my thigh. Who can I ask for his number who won't tattle to the entire town? Tough question since everyone on the island loves to gossip.

Good thing I have leverage.

"Hey, Harper," Blossom greets me.

"I need Kai's phone number and if you tell anyone I asked you for his number, I'm going to tell the entire island about the time you cheated at darts in my bar."

"I never cheated at darts," she claims.

"You bent the opponent's darts out of shape. I had to buy new darts." I didn't actually buy new darts. I had the old ones re-shaped since darts are not cheap.

"Ugh. You remind me of my husband using all your facts." She spits out the word facts, which would normally be hilarious since she uses facts to get her way as much as Jaxon does.

But I don't have time to dig into her hypocrisy. I have a Raider brother of my own to deal with. Kai isn't mine, but you get what I mean.

"Kai's number," I prompt.

"I would have given you Kai's number without the emotional blackmail."

"And then you would have told Jaxon and all of his brothers. The news would have spread across the island faster than Plank, the dirty-mouthed parrot, can fly."

"Whatever," she mutters and my phone beeps with a message. It's a contact for Kai.

"Thanks, Blossom," I say and hang up before she can ask any questions.

I stand and pace the room as I dial Kai's number.

"Hi, Slugger."

My brow wrinkles. "How do you know it's me?"

"It's this thing called modern technology. You may have heard of it."

I grunt. "Thanks for the reminder of how much older I am than you."

"Yes, you're ancient. Were dinosaurs as scary in person as they are in movies?"

"Ha. Ha. Aren't you funny early in the morning?"

"I'm funny all the time. Early in the morning, in the sunny afternoon, late at night."

I shiver at how he lowers his voice on 'late at night'. When did Kai Raider grow up and get a deep voice? Or those muscles on his chest? He's not a little boy anymore.

But then I remember why I'm calling.

"Who do you think you are?" I spit out my question.

"I'm Kai Raider."

"Don't be cute with me. You know what I mean."

"I do? You'll have to fill me in because I'm confused."

I open my mouth to lay into him but Dad yells, "Harper!" before I get the chance.

"I'm on the phone!"

"I can't find my Fruit Loops."

Those damn Fruit Loops. If I could, I'd contact the manufacturer and have the production stopped. They are more trouble than they're worth.

"Is that a man? Are you with another man, Harper?"

Another man? As if he has some kind of claim to me. I roll my eyes so hard at his indignation, I nearly give myself a headache.

"None of your business."

He growls. An honest to goodness growl.

"Harper!" Dad shouts again and I march out of my room to the kitchen. I easily find the Fruit Loops – it's possible they're in a spot too high for Dad to reach with his limited mobility – and plonk them on the table.

"There, Dad. Are you happy now?"

He doesn't respond. Merely reaches for the Fruit Loops. I blow out a breath. Is 'thank you' too much to ask for?

"Dad?" Kai asks. Shit. I'm still on the phone with him. "You live with your dad?"

I open the door to the patio and step outside. I shut the door behind me and march to the edge of the deck out of Dad's hearing range.

"Do not start with me."

"Sorry. I'm surprised, is all. Why do you live with your dad?"

"None of your business. I didn't phone you to discuss my living arrangements."

"Why did you phone me?"

"Because I don't appreciate you shoving your wealth in my face."

"Whoa. When did I shove my wealth in your face?"

"Are you serious right now? Do you have such an abundance of money you forgot what you did?"

Must be nice. Dad was a construction worker. He never made a ton of money, but we were comfortable before his stroke. Now? Now's another story entirely.

"I'm not some rich prick who sauntered onto the island and is throwing my wealth into everyone's face."

"You're not? You didn't pay several thousand dollars of bar tabs last night?"

"Oh."

"Yes, oh. Those bar tabs weren't supposed to be paid. I donate the top prize for the *Bootlegger Escape Room*. My donation is to pay the bar tabs of the winning team."

"I thought…"

"You thought what?" I ask when he trails off and doesn't finish his thought.

"Two teams tied this year. It was more money than normal."

Don't I know it. "What does this have to do with you?"

"Rhett may have mentioned you asked for a payment plan for your latest whiskey delivery."

Fuck. How could I forget those Raider brothers tell each other everything? Even when they're at each other's throats, they have each other's backs. Must be nice.

"My payment plan doesn't have anything to do with you."

"I thought it would be romantic if I paid for the bill. Some grand gesture."

Romantic? A grand gesture? I don't need some man to come riding in to save me. I'm doing fine all on my own. Who the smuggler does Kai Raider think he is?

I inhale a deep breath and let it out slowly but it doesn't help. My anger doesn't abate one bit.

"Buy a clue. Showing off your wealth isn't romantic. This is exactly my point about you. You've gotten everything handed to you. You don't know how it feels to have to work when you're throwing up all over the place, or to have to skip out on the senior trip in high school because you can't afford it. Everything has been handed to you on a silver platter."

"You're not being fair. My dad abandoned my family when I was ten."

"Welcome to the club. My mom died when I was sixteen."

"Shit. I didn't know. I'm sorry, Harper."

I ignore his sympathy. I didn't need it sixteen years ago. I don't need it now.

"I didn't phone you to share our sad stories. I phoned because what you did is not okay. Throwing money in my face is not okay. It's not romantic."

"Lesson learned."

"I doubt it," I murmur before hanging up.

And here I thought Kai helping out behind the bar last night was a step in the right direction. Silly me. Kai Raider will never grow up. He'll be fifty years old and still be immature. I want nothing to do with him.

I don't care how sexy those abs are or how warm his arms felt around me. He's not the man for me.

Chapter 8

"I'm not enjoying this self-realization stuff." ~ Kai

KAI

Miles picks up his surfboard and makes his way to me.

"What are you doing here this morning?" he asks as he plonks down next to me in the sand.

"Am I not allowed to observe my brother – one of the best surfers in the world – surf?"

"Uh oh. You're kissing my ass. What do you want?"

I play with the sand and watch it slip through my fingers. "Nothing."

He bumps my shoulder, and I shove him away. "You're soaking wet."

"I tend to get wet when I'm in the ocean."

"There's no reason to get me wet."

"Then, you should have gone to another brother for advice."

"I didn't come to you for advice."

"You're merely sitting here sulking because Harper turned you down again? I understand. Or, at least, I think I do. I've never had a woman turn me down before."

I narrow my eyes at him. "Don't lie to me. I know you tried hooking up with Hazel again."

"Hazel's in the past."

"But you want her in your future," I sing.

"I don't, but I know you want Harper in your future. You've been chasing after her for months now. Aren't you getting tired of being rejected?"

I frown. Being rejected is one thing, but the way Harper spoke to me this morning? It was hurtful. But was she right? Am I a spoiled brat?

"Do you think I'm a spoiled brat?"

Miles rears back. "Where did this come from?"

I contemplate lying to him but considering how angry Harper was, I doubt she's going to keep my 'gesture' to herself.

"I paid the bar bill for us and the brewery team last night."

His eyes widen as he whistles. "That must have been some bar tab."

Between my brothers buying rounds of shots for the bar and the brewery team buying beer for the bar, it was an enormous tab. I was worried about Harper paying for it.

"I was trying to do something nice for Harper."

He chuckles. "Go big or go home."

"Except she called me this morning. I thought she was going to blow an artery in her brain with how angry she was."

"She's stubborn and independent. What did you expect?"

For her to thank me. Preferably with her pretty lips I'm dying to taste. And if she decided to reward me with a strip tease, I wouldn't have minded in the least.

"I sure as shit didn't expect her to scream at me and claim I've been handed everything in life on a silver platter."

"Hmm…"

"Hmm? What hmm?"

Miles doesn't respond. He stares out into the ocean. I throw sand at him. "Explain yourself."

"I don't think you want to hear this."

"Tell me anyway."

"You have had it the easiest of the Raider brothers."

I growl. "Just because I'm the youngest, doesn't mean I had it the easiest."

"It's not about being the youngest. It's about timing."

"How is timing any different?"

He blows out a breath. "Eli and Rhett were older when Dad left."

I know this. They have more memories of Dad. I don't. I was ten when he left. My memories of Dad are clouded by all the underhanded remarks Mom and my brothers have made about him over the years.

"Dad didn't pay any child support, and Mom had six kids to feed. Eli worked several odd jobs to help pay the bills, and Rhett helped out in the house with cleaning and taking care of us."

What asshole doesn't pay child support for his six sons?

"I know all of this."

He cocks an eyebrow. "Do you?"

"What are you trying to say?"

"Did you have a job in high school?"

"No."

"Did you have to take care of your younger brothers when you were in high school?"

"You know I didn't."

"By the time you went to prom and were applying to colleges, Eli was already making good money with *Apparoo*."

Apparoo is the software company Eli founded with his college roommate. No one expected it to grow into a multi-billion-dollar company but it exceeded everyone's expectations. Especially Eli's.

"I still didn't get everything handed to me on a silver platter."

He shrugs, and I scowl. He's not being fair.

"If I got everything handed to me, you did, too."

"Wrong. I worked my ass off. I was out here surfing for hours before school and hours afterward."

"But it wasn't work. You loved it."

"It was totally work. And I didn't love it when my back was sore or when my face or hands were cut up from getting hit by my surfboard, but I still came out here every day to work on my sport. Not to mention all of the training outside of the surfing."

Damn. Is he right? I always considered Miles's surfing as a fun hobby he tried to make into a career until his shoulder injury in Hawaii ended his aspirations.

"I never thought of it this way."

"I'm not saying you're a spoiled brat or had everything handed to you. But you did have it easier than other people in this family."

My phone beeps with a message. I swear under my breath when I read it. "I need to go. Jaxon is losing his mind."

"Go. I'll catch you later in the office."

We stand and I study Miles. I always thought Miles was as much of a jokester and goofball as me. I never considered the amount of hours he trained to become a professional surfer.

"Later," I finally mutter before making my way to my car.

As I drive to the distillery, I consider everything Miles said. Miles, the charming surfer who doesn't take his job at the distillery seriously. Or so I thought.

"What's up?" I ask Jaxon when I stroll into my office fifteen minutes later.

"You were supposed to be here thirty minutes ago."

"I had things to do."

"What things? Did you meet with the delivery company to discuss our contract?"

"Meet with the delivery company?" What is he talking about?

He sighs. "These other things had nothing to do with your job as operations manager?"

I shrug since he already knows the answer to this question.

"This is why I asked Eli not to appoint you as the operations manager."

I scowl. "I'll be going to the ER to have the knife removed from my back now."

He frowns. "There's no knife in your back."

I forgot my nerdy brother doesn't understand metaphors. "You stabbed me in the back."

"I…" His eyes light with understanding and he trails off.

"You don't think I can do the job."

"No. I think you don't want to do this job. You're too young."

I'm sick of everyone pointing out my age. "What does my age have to do with anything? Eli was a director of *Apparoo* when he was my age."

"And he worked long hours to make the business a success. He didn't rely on other people to perform his work for him."

"I don't rely on other people to perform my work."

He raises his eyebrows. "I can't tell if you are this unaware or if you're lying."

I rear back. "Lying? Are you saying I'm a liar?"

"Unaware it is," he mumbles under his breath.

"Look," I begin, "I've had enough of hard truths for one day. Can we discuss this another time?"

"No, we can't. Blossom and I want to start having children. I plan to help raise my children. I won't be an absent father."

Unlike our own father. "Good for you."

He purses his lips. "You don't understand. I can't be home with my children if I'm doing your job as well as mine."

"You don't do my job."

"I can prove it to you." He drops a pile of paper onto my desk.

"What's this?"

"I've detailed every task required of the master distiller and the operations manager. I've also provided examples of when I did your job."

I thumb through the document. "I don't know what the big deal is."

He growls. "The big deal is you're being paid to be the operations manager for *Buccaneer's Distillery* but you are not performing the job. I understand you're young and want to have fun. Maybe it's time for you to quit."

I pause rifling through the document to meet his gaze. Is he serious? He can't possibly be serious. When Eli founded the distillery, he made it clear all managerial positions would be held by his brothers – no outsiders allowed.

"You want me to quit?"

"No. I want you to grow up and do your job."

"I'm not a child."

He points to the document. "Then, prove it. Do your job. If you need help understanding any tasks, feel free to ask me. But I will no longer be doing your job for you."

"And if I don't?"

He stands. "I've already spoken to Eli."

Guess there are now two knives I need to have removed from my back.

"What? He didn't mention anything to me."

"Because he doesn't want to believe his beloved baby brother is a slacker."

"I'm not a slacker."

His brow wrinkles. "I believe I used the term correctly. Slacker. A person who avoids work or effort."

"I'm not a slacker," I repeat.

He points to the stack of paper. "Prove it."

He spins on his heel and marches away. I collapse in my chair. What a day. I reach for my phone, intent on messaging Zane with a request we get out of here and have some fun, but pause with my finger on the send button.

When Dad abandoned us, I decided life was too short to be serious. Maybe I went too far. Maybe I have become a slacker – allowing Jaxon to do my work.

I reach for the document. A little read couldn't hurt.

Chapter 9

"I'm done with grass. We're installing AstroTurf and calling it a day." ~ Harper

HARPER

The door to my office flies open and I quickly click away from the book website. I'm trying to find my next romantic suspense book to read. I love reading romance. So sue me.

"Hey, boss," Sloane says. "The beer delivery is here."

I stand. "Thanks."

"I can handle it."

"You're the only person behind the bar this afternoon. I need you there."

"Okay," she agrees but she looks like I kicked her puppy.

I frown as she leaves. Sloane wants more responsibility but every time I give it to her, she flakes on me. The last time she said she'd open up early for a delivery of new glassware, she 'forgot' about it and I ended up taking delivery in my pajamas. Not my finest moment.

I make my way to the rear entrance and open the door.

"Hey," I greet Chloe. "I didn't expect you."

Chloe is the bar and restaurant manager for *Five Fathoms Brewing*, the local brewery on Smuggler's Hideaway. I exclusively stock *Five Fathoms* beer. Not only do I want to support a local company – especially one owned and operated by five women – but their beer is fantastic.

"I volunteered."

I narrow my eyes at her. "You volunteered or you were volunteered?"

Her nose wrinkles. "What's the difference?"

"The difference is I need to know what you did."

She rolls her eyes. "No one can handle a joke anymore."

"What did you do?"

"I may have dressed up as a mermaid ghost and haunted the brewery."

"What happened?"

"Blossom screamed and went running. Straight into Paisley, who fell."

I gasp. Paisley's pregnant. "Is she okay?"

"She's fine. Doesn't have a scratch on her, but Eli went overprotective future girl daddy on me."

"Girl daddy? Is Paisley having a girl?"

"Crap on a mermaid cracker. I'm not supposed to tell."

I zip my lips. "I don't have anyone to tell."

She snorts. "You have an entire bar of patrons you can spill the beans to."

"You're confused. It's my job to learn the secrets of the island from my patrons. Not the other way around."

The driver saunters toward me with a clipboard. "Here you go."

He hands me the clipboard but my phone rings before I have a chance to look at it. "Excuse me."

"Hi Jade," I greet my neighbor. "Please tell me Dad isn't watering your flowers with his urine again."

"Oh, honey."

My heart stops at the sympathy clear to hear in her voice. "What's wrong? What happened? Is Dad okay?"

"You need to come home."

"On my way."

I'm already running before I hang up.

"I'll handle the delivery," Chloe shouts from behind me. I wave to acknowledge her.

I run all the way home. Why didn't I drive today? I usually drive, but I decided it was a lovely day for a walk. No more. I won't be caught without my car again.

I round the corner of my street and notice a crowd has gathered on my front lawn. I shove my way through everyone to reach Dad, who's sitting on the grass.

"What's going on? What happened?"

"The lawn mower attacked me."

"The lawn mower? What were you doing with the lawn mower?" Dad shouldn't be mowing the lawn. He needs a cane to walk for smuggler's sake! "Jade's son, Adrian, mows the lawn."

"Look at the lawn. He hasn't mowed in weeks."

"I'm sorry." Jade wrings her hands. "Adrian is away at rugby camp. He's supposed to come home on the weekends, but he's having a good time and…"

I hold up my hand to stop her. "This is not your fault, Jade."

I offer Dad my hand. "Let's get you up and in the house."

He raises his left arm and I notice it's bent at a strange angle. This is not good since his right arm never fully recovered from his stroke.

How am I going to get him in the car and drive him to the hospital? I don't want to use an ambulance. Ambulance rides are not covered in my insurance.

A siren wails. Too late.

But when I glance over my shoulder, it's not an ambulance arriving. It's a police car. Lucas, Chloe's husband, folds out of the police vehicle and makes his way to me.

"Chloe rang me. She thought you might need help."

"Thank the smugglers for mermaid ghosts," I mutter.

"Mermaid ghosts?" Dad asks. "I'm not the one who needs help."

"Dad," I grumble. "We're going to the hospital. You need to have your arm x-rayed."

"Stupid lawnmower. I told you to buy a riding lawnmower."

"Our yard is the size of a postage stamp. We don't need a riding lawnmower."

"And you don't need to be paying some kid to mow."

"I am not doing this with you now, Dad." I meet Lucas's gaze. "Can you help me get him in my car?"

"I got this," he says before kneeling next to my dad. "How do you feel about a ride in a police car?"

"Haven't been in a police car in ages. Will you put on the sirens and lights?"

"I can even put you in the back seat."

"Deal."

Lucas makes it appear easy when he picks up my dad, unlike the last time I tried to carry my dad and nearly gave myself a hernia.

I rush to follow them but Jade stops me with a hand on my arm. "I'll put the lawnmower away."

Only then do I notice the lawnmower laying on its side. "Thanks, Jade. And thanks for the call."

"Of course," she says before nudging me toward the police car where Lucas is setting Dad in the rear seat.

"Did you cuff him?" I ask Lucas.

Dad scowls. "No need to cuff me when I have one useless arm."

I was joking, but Dad isn't. He's a proud man and not being able to work since his stroke doesn't sit well with him. He doesn't want to be a burden. He's my dad. He'll never be a burden. A pain in my ass, on the other hand? For sure.

I settle into the front seat. Lucas sits next to me before switching on the lights and sirens.

"Whoo-hoo!" Dad shouts from the back seat.

It's been such a long time since I heard my dad excited about anything. I should have asked Lucas to give him a ride before now. Instead of waiting until he's injured.

We weave through the tourist traffic in Smuggler's Rest until we're on the road toward Rogue's Landing. The hospital is halfway between the two main towns on the island.

"You enjoying the ride, Dad?" I ask, but when I glance over my shoulder, I notice he's slumped over. "Dad!" He doesn't respond.

"Lucas!" I shriek. "He's unconscious."

"Hold on, Harper. We're nearly there." He alerts the hospital staff that we're three minutes out and will be arriving with an unresponsive male.

An unresponsive male? I bite my lip and dig my fingernails into my palms to steady myself. I've been here before when Dad had his stroke.

Is he having another stroke? Can a fall cause a stroke in a stroke victim? All the knowledge I have about strokes disappears in a puff of air from my mind. I can't remember anything.

Lucas pats my thigh. "Deep breaths, Harper. Deep breaths. I don't need you passing out, too."

I nod and force myself to inhale a deep breath. I hold for three seconds before letting it out. I inhale another breath but we arrive at the hospital before I've managed to calm myself down.

When Lucas screeches to a halt in front of the emergency room, I jump out of the vehicle.

"Help! I need help!"

Four people rush out of the emergency room with a stretcher. "It's my dad."

Lucas lifts Dad out of the car and on to the stretcher. They wheel him into the hospital and I rush to follow. A security guard blocks me. He nods to the registration desk.

"But—"

Lucas steers me toward the desk. "Let them do their job."

"But—"

"You'll be in their way. They know what they're doing. Your dad is in good hands."

The receptionist hands me a clipboard to fill out. "You need to…"

"I know the drill."

She pats my arm. "He's in good hands."

Lucas guides me away from the desk. "Do you need me to phone anyone?"

"There's no one. It's just me and Dad."

"A friend?"

I shake my head. Who has time for friends when you're operating a business and caring for your father? Not me.

"Do you want me to stay with you? My shift is almost over."

I wave him away. "I'll be fine. This isn't my first rodeo."

He frowns. "If you're sure."

I force a smile. "Thanks for your help getting him here. I don't know what I would have done without you."

"You would have figured it out."

True. I always do.

He squeezes my hand before making his way across the waiting room to the exit. Once he's gone, I collapse in a chair and bury my face in my hands.

What am I going to do? I can't live without Dad. I can't lose another parent. He's all I have.

Chapter 10

"Sexy distraction needed? I'm on my way." ~ Kai

KAI

My phone rings and I frown at the caller ID – *Smuggler's Hideaway Police Station.*

"I didn't do it and I was with my brothers the entire time," I answer the phone.

"It's Lucas."

"Officer Fellows, how can I assist you today?" I don't bother pretending I don't know who Lucas is. It would be a lie and, while I'm a proficient liar, lying to the police never works out.

"Harper's at the emergency room."

My stomach drops and my heart clenches. "What? What happened? Is she okay? Of course, she's not okay. She's at the hospital."

"Calm down, Raider. She's fine. Her dad fell."

I blow out a breath. "Okay. Good. Well, not good. How's her dad?"

"Unknown."

"Shit. Should I go? Never mind. I'm going." I jump to my feet, grab my keys, and rush for the door.

"Don't make me regret phoning you, Raider."

"You won't."

Thankfully, the hospital isn't far from the distillery. I make it there in less than five minutes. I rush inside and scan the room for Harper. She's sitting in the corner with her face in her hands. No.

I sit next to her. "Hey, Harper."

She whips her head up. "What are you doing here?"

"I heard you were here and was worried."

"This town," she mutters before raising her voice. "I'm fine. Go home."

"I'm not going anywhere."

"Don't you have some shenanigans to pull?"

I turn my pockets inside out to show her they're empty. "I'm all out of shenanigans."

"I'm serious, Kai. I'm fine."

"What about your dad?"

Her face crumbles. "I don't know. They haven't told me anything."

"I'll ask."

"They won't tell you anything."

"I'm going to try anyway." I kiss her cheek before standing and sauntering to the reception desk. I give the receptionist – an elderly woman named Moira, whom I've met a time or two – my biggest smile.

"No," she says before I can speak.

"You don't know what my question is."

She lifts an eyebrow. "But I do know you, Kai Raider. And you're not bleeding or vomiting. Have a seat and wait."

I open my mouth to question her more but notice Dr. Allens walking my way. My smile widens. "Dr. Allens."

She sighs. "Who's injured today?"

"No one. I'm actually worried about my friend's dad. She's been waiting a while and is really worried."

I motion toward Harper, who is now pacing the waiting room.

"This is Henry's daughter?"

"Yes," I say, although I don't know Harper's dad's name. I'm guessing he's the only man with a worried daughter in the ER at the moment.

"She can come through."

"Harper." I motion her over and she rushes to me.

"Follow me," Dr. Allens says.

I capture Harper's hand and she squeezes. Squeeze as hard as you want, Harper. I'm here and I'm not leaving you, no matter how many times you ask me to.

Dr. Allens opens a door and motions us inside. There's a man asleep on the bed. He's hooked up to various machines and has a cast on one arm.

Harper drops my hand and rushes to him. "Why is he unconscious?"

"He's not unconscious," the doctor explains. "He's sleeping. We gave him a powerful dose of painkillers."

"Powerful dose? Was he in a lot of pain? What's wrong?"

The doctor motions to his arm. "He broke his arm and pulled his shoulder out of the joint."

I wince. My shoulder's been pulled out of the joint once. It was more painful than breaking it. "Ouch."

"Can I take him home? Does he need to stay overnight? He's going to lose his mind if he has to stay in the hospital overnight."

Dr. Allens chuckles. "He told me in no uncertain terminology he was not staying overnight, no matter what."

Harper sighs. "That's my dad for you."

"He should be ready to go in an hour."

"Okay." She nods as she searches for a chair. "I'll wait with him."

"Go away," her dad mumbles. "Let me sleep in peace."

"Dad!" She smiles down at him. "You're okay."

He scowls. "My arm is broken."

"Remember what you told me when I broke my arm in fourth grade?"

"What?"

"Better a broken arm than a broken ass."

I bite my tongue before I laugh. I think I'm going to like Henry.

"I'm..." Henry breaks off to yawn. "I'm going to sleep for a while."

Dr. Allens opens the door. "Come on. You can handle his paperwork while he sleeps."

Harper bites her lip as she contemplates her dad. She's obviously reluctant to leave him alone. I place my hand on her lower back and steer her toward the door. "He's not going anywhere."

When we reach the hallway, I thank Dr. Allens and she rushes off without a backward glance.

"Shall we get a coffee while we wait? The cafeteria coffee isn't bad. It's not Parker's coffee, but it's drinkable."

"I don't want to leave Dad."

"Not a problem," I say and stop in front of Moira. "We're going for a coffee in the cafeteria. Can you let us know if anything changes with Harper's dad?"

She directs her answer to Harper. "Of course, honey. You go have a break."

Harper wrings her hands but I grasp one and lead her to the cafeteria. I wait until we're seated with our coffees before I speak again.

"It's a broken arm. He'll recover."

"You don't get it. It's the only arm he can use."

Is he missing an arm? "What?"

"There's a reason I live with my dad and it's not because I'm young and immature."

The blow hits me, but I ignore the pain in my chest. "Why?"

"Ugh. Why do you want to know this?"

I reach across the table to clasp her hand. "I want to know everything about you, Harper."

"Maybe when you realize how boring my life is, you'll leave me alone."

"Nothing about you could be boring."

"Really? I don't have millions of dollars to jet off to fancy locations for vacation."

"Neither do I."

"Or a billionaire brother to rely on."

I don't rely on Eli. Except he gave me a job which pays more than most twenty-four-year-olds earn. A job Jaxon doesn't think I'm qualified for.

I shove those thoughts away. Harper isn't going to distract me from the matter at hand.

"You can try and distract me for as long as you want. I have five brothers. I'm used to distraction."

She tugs her hand from mine. I frown. I was enjoying feeling her small hand in mine. She has callouses from how hard she works but they don't bother me. They remind me of how strong she is. I suspect she's much stronger than I know.

"Fine." She huffs. "A year after my mom died, my dad had a stroke. He worked hard in rehab to regain mobility, but his right arm and leg never recovered. He had to quit working. It's hard to construct buildings when you have to use a cane to walk and your right arm doesn't work properly."

I was correct. Harper is much stronger than I knew.

"And now you take care of him."

"As much as he'll allow me to. He's stubborn."

I snort. "A family trait."

She glares at me. "I'm not stubborn."

"Of course not, Slugger."

"I didn't slug anyone."

"Because I stopped you."

"You did not stop me."

"No?" I feign innocence. "You weren't distracted by my sexy abs and forgot you were in the middle of a fight?"

She narrows her eyes at me. "Sexy abs?"

I inch my t-shirt up. "I can show you again in case you forgot."

"No!" She squeals. "No stripping in the hospital."

I drop my shirt with a sigh. "Boring but okay."

"I told you I was boring. Hold on. Are you wearing glitter?"

I groan. "I'm going to kill my brothers."

"What did they do?"

"They glitter bombed me."

She giggles and the sound fills me with warmth. Harper should laugh more. She needs more fun in her life. Not to worry. I'm on the job.

"I amend my question. What did you do?"

I raise my hands in the air. "I'm innocent of all charges."

She barks out a laugh. "Kai Raider innocent? You haven't been innocent a day in your life."

I bat my eyelashes. "I was an adorable baby."

"All babies are adorable."

"Do you want children?"

She motions to the room. "Do you not see where we are? I can barely handle my life as it is."

"It's not your fault your dad fell."

"I should have hidden the lawnmower."

"Lawnmower?"

"Dad didn't 'approve' of the neighbor kid's mowing and decided to handle the task himself."

"With one working arm and a cane?"

"Told you he was stubborn."

"It's still not your fault he was injured."

She blows out a breath. "I feel responsible."

"You can't be responsible for everything and everyone."

"Oh yeah? Watch me."

I drain my coffee and gather our mugs before standing. "Come on, my little responsible slugger. Let's go bust your dad out of the hospital."

"Responsible and slugger don't go together," she says as she follows me.

I raise a brow. "Really? Have you looked in the mirror lately?" I point at her. "Responsible slugger."

"I need to buy you a dictionary."

"Good idea. I need a doorstop."

She shakes her head but her lips are turned up and there's no longer brackets around her eyes. She might not realize it yet, but I'm good for her. I can be her distraction when she needs one.

I can be a whole lot more.

Patience, Kai. Patience. I've chiseled a crack into the ice surrounding Harper's heart. I'll keep chiseling until it breaks wide open and she lets me in. She's worth the effort.

Chapter 11

"I got this." ~ Harper

HARPER

"I don't need your help," I tell Kai for the millionth time.

He smiles at me, and I ignore how my stomach warms in response. Don't you dare sprout butterflies now, stomach, or we will no longer be friends.

"Your chariot awaits, Daddy Poole." He bows to my dad, and my dad? He actually chuckles.

"I don't need a wheelchair," he grumbles but there's less anger in his voice than when I usually try to get him into a wheelchair.

"Sorry, daddy-o. It's a hospital policy. Trust me. I know. I'm a regular here." He winks and Dad settles himself in the wheelchair without any further complaints. What the hell? Is Kai a miracle worker?

Kai wheels Dad toward the exit, and I rush to follow them. "Wait. Our ride isn't here yet."

Kai motions to a large SUV. "Your ride has arrived."

"You don't have to drive us home. I can order a ride from the ride-share app."

Kai ignores me and helps Dad into the front seat of his SUV.

"Kai," I growl as he passes me with the empty wheelchair. "I'm serious. We don't need your help."

"Harper Poole, I am well aware you can handle everything in your life on your own. But you don't have to."

I bristle. "I can handle everything."

"I know, Slugger. I just said the same thing. Now, get in there before your dad commandeers my radio station." He tweaks my nose before rushing off to return the wheelchair to the hospital.

I climb into the back seat. And I do mean climb. This SUV is made for giants. I'm barely five-foot-five-inches tall. Okay, fine. I'm actually five-three and a half.

"You have to have this gigantic vehicle," I complain to Kai when he returns.

"In case you haven't noticed, I'm a gigantic man." He winks at me via the rearview mirror and I groan. I forgot about his love of cheesy lines.

"We're in Smuggler's Rest on Pirate's Lane," I tell Kai when he begins to drive.

"I know where you live, Harper."

"Are you two going to flirt the entire drive, or is a little quiet too much for an old man to ask?" Dad gripes.

"We are not flirting."

Kai chuckles. "We're totally flirting."

"Your mom and I used to bicker all the time until she finally realized she loved me."

"I thought you fell in love instantly."

Dad grunts. "I did. Your mom took a bit of convincing."

"I know what you mean," Kai mumbles.

My heart gallops in my chest at his words. Is Kai actually serious about me? He's a player. He picks up and drops women in the blink of an eye. He's merely flirting with me because he thinks I'm playing hard to get. Or is he?

We arrive at our house and I rush inside to get Dad's wheelchair.

"I don't need a damn wheelchair," Dad complains when I return.

I inhale a deep breath to calm my irritation before I lash out at Dad. I get it. He doesn't want to be seen as weak. He used to be a big, strong construction worker before his stroke.

It's been fifteen years but he still hasn't adjusted to his situation. I can't blame him. I wouldn't adjust well to not having control over an arm and leg either.

"How else are you going to get into the house? You can't use your cane."

Dad glares at his broken arm and swears under his breath.

"I can carry you if you prefer," Kai offers.

"I'm not a baby," Dad mutters.

"Wheelchair it is then," Kai says before placing Dad in the wheelchair. He rolls the chair to the front and frowns. "You have stairs."

"Thank you, Captain Obvious."

"I just thought..." He trails off. "Never mind." He hoists Dad's chair with Dad in it and carries it up the four steps.

My mouth gapes open. How the hell did he lift Dad and the chair? Together, they weigh more than two hundred pounds. I usually drag the wheelchair up the steps and am coated in sweat by the time I'm finished.

"Stop staring at my muscles and open the door, Slugger."

"I wasn't..." I clear my throat before I can finish the lie.

Of course, I was staring at his muscles. His biceps are bulging from his efforts, and his t-shirt is straining over his chest. When did little Kai – the brat who was always trying to sneak into *Rumrunner* before he was of age – grow those muscles?

I hurry to the front door and unlock it. Kai wheels Dad inside.

"I got this." I nudge Kai out of the way and push Dad the rest of the way to his bedroom.

"I'm not a baby. I don't need a nap."

I wish I had time for a nap. But no one's asking me.

"The doctor said you'd be tired from the pain meds."

"I'm not..." A yawn cuts him off.

I raise an eyebrow at him.

"Fine. I'm tired. But it's because of the pain meds. Not because I'm a baby."

"Of course not."

I help him into bed. "You good?"

His response? A snore. I guess he's good.

I pause at the door to study him. In his sleep, he appears peaceful. Unlike when he's awake and fighting me on every-damn-thing.

I shut the door behind me and tiptoe down the hallway. Dad's usually a light sleeper. I never could get away with sneaking into the house late when I was a teenager.

I skid to a halt at the opening to the living room. Kai is sitting on the couch.

"What are you still doing here?"

"Waiting for you."

"Waiting for me? Kai." I sigh. "I can't deal with any lame pick-up lines right now."

He clutches his chest. "My pick-up lines are lame? Harsh."

I roll my eyes. "What do you want?"

"I want to check how you're doing."

"Me?" I tap my chest. "I'm fine. I'm not the one who wrenched my shoulder out of the socket and broke my only useable arm."

"I know you're fine physically." His gaze rakes over me and I lock my limbs before I squirm under his scrutiny. "But what about mentally? You have a lot going on."

"Tell me about it," I mutter.

"Come. Sit down." He motions me forward. "I made you coffee."

"You made me coffee?" He offers me a mug but I shake my head.

"It won't bite you." He waggles his eyebrows. "Unlike me."

I grunt. "There's Mr. Lame Pick-up Line."

"Got you to smile, though, didn't I?"

I realize I am indeed smiling and scowl. "Whatever." I snag the mug from him. "Huh. This isn't bad."

"Unless I poisoned you."

"What?" I nearly spit out my coffee until I realize Kai's laughing. "Can you ever be serious?"

"Yes." He nods. "Let's get serious. You need help."

"Help? What do you mean?" I know exactly what he means, but my mind is too tired to think of another way to delay this conversation.

Kai motions down the hallway. "Your dad can't get around on his own until his cast is off and his arm and shoulder are healed."

"I know."

"How are you going to manage the bar and be here for your dad?"

I bristle. This is my problem to solve. Not his. "I'll figure something out. The neighbors usually pitch in to help."

"You should hire a caretaker."

I glare at him. "I'm not hiring a caretaker. Dad took care of Mom when she was sick. I can care for him."

"It's sweet you want to handle this on your own, but you don't have to."

Yes, I do. I can't afford to hire a caretaker. I'm barely managing to pay my bills as it is.

"This isn't any of your business."

"You're my friend, Harper. I care about you. I don't enjoy seeing you struggle."

I ignore how warm and fuzzy the words 'I care about you' make me feel. It's been too long since anyone said they cared about me. I can't allow myself to be distracted. I won't allow myself to be intimidated. I've got this.

"I'm not struggling. I'm managing."

"No. You *were* managing. Your dad's accident is not a little bump in the road. With both of his arms compromised, he can no longer cook, dress, or do any of the day-to-day tasks he used to handle."

"What do you know about it?"

"I have five brothers who think daring each other is a sign of love. I can't count the number of broken bones we've suffered. And when someone broke an arm or a leg, we stepped in to help each other. This is what families do."

Nice for him. I don't have any family besides Dad. It's just the two of us.

"Which is what I'm doing. I'm helping my dad."

He blows out a breath. "You also need help."

I stand and walk to the door. "Thank you for your help today, but I've got it from here." When he doesn't move, I open the door.

"Stubborn woman," he mutters before standing and marching to me. "Know this, Harper, I am not done with this conversation."

"Too bad. I am."

He scowls before kissing my hair and leaving.

I shut the door behind him and sink to the floor. What am I going to do? How am I going to manage the bar and take care of Dad?

Kai wants to help.

I ignore the thought. Kai will lose interest in me and my problems soon enough. The man's a player. And what twenty-year-old wants to be saddled with my problems? None.

Chapter 12

"May the most stubborn person win!" ~ *Kai*

KAI

I park my SUV in Harper's driveway. "I should probably tell you something before we go inside."

"Oh, man, what is it?" Carl asks. "Are they nudists? I can handle nudists. I am a nurse after all."

I chuckle. "Not nudists."

Although I wouldn't mind watching Harper race around the house naked. Her breasts would bounce and I'm certain those ass cheeks I want to spank would be a thing of beauty.

"Are they into BDSM? I'm okay with it as long as I don't have to watch. The last couple asked me to watch and I walked away. No, thank you."

"It's a father and his daughter."

"She doesn't abuse him, does she? I will not hesitate to contact the police. I don't care how many pots she throws at me or how many times she chases me with a knife. I'm fast and I don't abide elderly abuse."

"When this assignment is finished, we are sitting down and having a beer. You have some stories to tell."

"Sorry. Client confidentiality."

I grin at his answer. I knew I chose right when I picked Carl.

"Here's the thing. Harper and Henry don't know you're coming."

His eyes narrow. "Don't know, I'm coming, as in we're early?"

"Ah, no." I drag a hand through my hair. "They don't know I hired you."

His eyes widen. "I better get paid."

"You'll get paid. I guarantee it."

"Okay, let's go."

"You're not worried?"

He snorts. "You're the one who should be worried."

Damn. Is he right? Have I overstepped? The same way I did when I paid off those bar tabs? No, this is different. I'm not shoving my wealth into her face. I'm helping her out during a difficult time.

The front door opens and Harper steps out onto the porch. Procrastination time is done.

"What are you doing here?" she asks when we approach the door. "And who's this?"

"Close the damn door, Harper," her dad shouts from inside. "You're letting all the flies in."

"This is Carl." I motion to him. "He's your new nurse."

Her eyes narrow to tiny slits. "My new nurse? I didn't hire a nurse."

"I did it for you. I know how busy you are. Carl has great references. I'll send you an email with all of his information."

"Nice to meet you." Carl extends his hand. I hold my breath as I wait for Harper's response. She's grumpy, but she's not rude. I sigh in relief when she shakes his hand.

"I'm Harper."

"Shall we go inside and meet the patient?" I ask but I don't wait for Harper to respond before opening the door and ushering everyone inside.

"I'm not a patient," Henry says.

"Hi, Henry," I greet. "This is Carl. He's a nurse. He's going to help you get around while your arm recovers."

Henry glares at Carl. "I'm not disabled."

"You're more stubborn than your daughter."

Henry grunts. "Have you met Harper? She's the most stubborn daughter in the world."

I chuckle. "I've met her. I know."

Harper throws her hands in the air. "Can we stop discussing how stubborn I am and move on to how you hired a nurse without letting me know?"

"You hired the nurse?" Henry asks.

I lean close to whisper to him, "I figured you might want a man to help you get to the bathroom and change your clothes."

"Thank fuck. Carl, I need to use the facilities."

Carl brings over the wheelchair and helps Henry into it before wheeling him down the hallway.

I wait until the door is closed behind them before facing Harper. "Let it out."

She doesn't hesitate. "I cannot believe you." I start toward the kitchen. "Where do you think you're going?"

"I'm making us coffee. I assume this is going to take a while."

Her chest heaves as her cheeks darken in anger. "No, this won't take a while. You need to leave and take your nurse with you, too. This is worse than paying off the bar tab. You can't just buy me a nurse."

I notice the dishes piled up in the sink. "Do you have a dishwasher?"

"Hello! Are you listening to me?"

"Everyone's listening to you," Henry shouts from the bathroom. "The entire neighborhood can hear you!"

I open and close drawers.

"What are you doing now?"

"Searching for a dishwasher."

"You're going to be searching for a long time since we don't have one."

I want to buy her one, but considering how much she's freaking out about the nurse, I table the thought. I roll up my sleeves before filling the sink with water. I add some dishwasher soap.

"I'm dreaming. This is some crazy dream due to lack of sleep."

I latch onto the lack of sleep. "This is why I'm trying to help. You can't do it all."

"And you can't buy me a nurse to solve all my problems," she grits out. "This is why I'm not interested in going out on a date with you. I want a partner who listens to me."

"Sorry, Slugger, but I'm not sorry. You're already working yourself to death. I won't allow someone I care for to hurt herself."

"And your solution was to buy me a caretaker? This is not you taking care of me. This is you rolling right over my wishes."

I leave the dishes in the sink and prowl toward her. She backs up until she bumps into the kitchen counter. I slam my hands on the counter next to her hips – caging her in.

"What do you want, Harper? You know you can't possibly look after your dad round-the-clock while managing *Rumrunner*. What is your solution? Because from where I'm standing, you are out of options."

"Options?" She snorts. "I haven't had options since Mom died and Dad had his stroke."

Her eyes fill with pain and I palm her cheek. "Reach out and grasp the hand I'm offering you, Harper."

"I don't want your charity."

"Good. Because you aren't getting it. You're paying for the nurse."

"What? I can't afford a nurse. How am I going to manage?" She fists her hands in my t-shirt. "I can't, Kai. There's no more money."

"No money? I don't understand. *Rumrunner* is packed whenever I'm there."

Her cheeks flush as a muscle ticks in her jaw. I assume she won't answer but she does.

"The monthly loan payments for the bar are substantial."

I want to ask more questions, but she's in full-on stubborn mode.

I frame her face with my hands. "It doesn't matter. Your dad is a vet. He can get VA benefits."

"But…"

I place a finger over her lips. "I did some research. I've got all the forms for you to fill out in my vehicle."

Her bottom lip trembles and she sniffs. "Don't cry, Harper."

"I can't help it. No one's been this nice to me since Mom was alive."

A tear escapes and I wipe it away. "You're breaking my heart, Harper."

"I'm sorry. I can't help it. It's been a lot. Mom and then Dad and—"

I press my lips to hers. I only meant to stop her from reeling out of control, but the second I feel her soft lips against mine, I'm lost. I've waited months to touch Harper. Months to feel her lips against mine.

She sighs and I plunge my tongue into her mouth. I thought I was lost before. Now, I am well and truly lost. Because Harper tastes of vanilla and beer. It's heaven. She's heaven.

She leans her body against mine. I groan at the feel of her breasts pressing against my chest. I glide my hands down her side to her hips. I grasp them and pick her up and place her on the counter. She doesn't hesitate to wrap her legs around my waist.

My cock – hard and wanting – throbs in my jeans. It urges me to throw caution to the wind and take Harper right here, right now.

"Ahem."

"AHEM!"

I rip my mouth away from Harper to glance over my shoulder.

Carl smirks at me. "I thought I'd warn you before Henry walked in on you."

"I can't walk!" Henry shouts from behind him. "But I can hear."

I chuckle, but Harper groans and buries her face in my chest. "This is not happening."

"Sorry, Slugger, this is happening."

Her head whips up and she glares at me. "This." She motions between us. "Isn't happening."

I wink. "Don't worry. I'll convince you otherwise."

"Kai," she growls.

I help her down from the kitchen counter. "Let me get the paperwork. It's a lot, but there's a helpline if you get stuck or I can drive you to the nearest VA office to get their help."

She slaps my chest. "Stop being nice. It's annoying."

"You wish it was annoying." I wink at her before sauntering out of the kitchen.

I nearly collide with Henry, who's sitting in his wheelchair near the kitchen table. He gives me a thumbs-up.

"You can give the paperwork to Carl," Harper shouts from the kitchen.

She thinks she can avoid me. It's cute. There's no way I'll let her avoid me, especially since I've managed to crack the ice around her heart wide open. She'll try repairing the crack but I'll chisel it away bit by bit until she realizes there's no need to protect herself from me.

Chapter 13

"I hate being wrong." ~ Harper

HARPER

"Good afternoon, Harper," Carl greets when I let him into the house.

"Dad's taking a nap. His pain meds knocked him out. I'm late for work but if you need anything, call me. My cell number and the number for the bar are on the refrigerator."

"I've got everything under control. I'll see you when you get off work."

"It'll be late."

"Yes, I understand a bar owner doesn't get off work at five in the afternoon."

I ignore the obvious sarcasm and barrel on. "I made the bed in the guest room up in case you want to sleep. You don't need to stay up if Dad's in bed."

He squeezes my shoulder. "I promise everything will be okay."

I hesitate. This is my first time leaving Carl alone with Dad. We spent the day yesterday going over Dad's routine and getting to know each other.

I know Carl is competent – I might have insisted he show me his qualifications – but this is my dad. I've never left him alone with anyone for more than an hour – let alone a stranger from the mainland.

"Harper, go to work."

I bite my bottom lip. I should be the one to stay with Dad. He's my responsibility. What kind of person am I, leaving the care of my family to a stranger?

"You can always have one of your nosey neighbors check on me if you're worried."

"I don't have nosey neighbors."

It's a lie. My neighbors are totally nosey. In fact, Jade is peeking through her garage window at us now. I wave to her and she gives me a thumbs-up.

I notice the time. I'm late. I can't stand in the doorway all day. No one wins then.

"I'm going," I say and manage to drag myself out the door.

I arrive at work five minutes later. Five minutes. I can be home in five minutes if Dad needs me. If Carl flakes and runs off. Although, the more likely scenario is Dad chasing Carl off.

My phone beeps with a message from Stud Muffin. Stud Muffin? I don't have anyone listed in my contacts under Stud Muffin.

How is Carl working out?
Who is this?

Kai.

Did you change your name to Stud Muffin in my contacts?

You're welcome.

I'm changing it back to Interfering Man-Child.

Pretty sure I proved I'm not a child yesterday.

My body warms and I fan myself at the reminder of yesterday. I've thought of my kiss with Kai about a million times since it happened. Our kiss was sexier than any kiss I've read about in a book before. And I've read plenty of kissing scenes, considering my addiction to romance novels.

I don't know what you're talking about.

I'm happy to give you a reminder.

Some of us have to work.

If you change your mind, I'll be at Mermaid Karaoke with my brothers later. Feel free to stop by.

Good reminder. Kai is a player. And I never learned how to share my toys. I have no desire to be with a man who doesn't understand the word monogamy. I don't care how much my toes curled during our kiss.

I won't.

I shove my phone in my pocket before I'm tempted to keep texting with Kai. I have work to do.

The rear door flies open and Sloane rushes inside.

"What are you doing here?"

"You said you need help with the inventory."

"And you said you couldn't help because you can't leave Boozer alone for too long."

She shrugs. "I found a doggy walker."

I raise my eyebrow. "You found a doggy walker? I've been asking you to find one for years."

"Kai found one for me. She's great. She can't have a dog of her own because her husband's allergic, but she loves dogs. She's going to the beach with him. Boozer is going to love her more than me."

I hold up a hand. "Did you say Kai found your doggy walker?"

"Yep. He phoned me the other day and set everything up." She frowns at me. "What's wrong? You're Siren's Scowl is blaring at me."

"Kai won't stop interfering in my life."

"Oh yeah?" She inches closer. "How is he interfering in your life?"

I groan. "How big is the jackpot?"

She blinks her eyes. "I don't know what you're referring to."

"The jackpot for whoever wins the bet about when Kai and I will get together. How big is it?"

"Nope. Not telling." She zips her lips.

I tap my foot, cross my arms over my chest, and give her my best Siren's Scowl.

"No fair! You can't give me the look. No one can resist the look."

"How big is the jackpot?"

"It's big," she bursts out. "Every time someone's date passes, the money is rolled over into a new bet."

My nostrils flare. "How long have people on this island been betting on me behind my back?"

"It's not behind your back. Everyone just wants you to be happy. You work really hard at the bar and then take care of your father at home."

"I'm about done with everyone complaining I work too hard."

"People care about you, Harper. Is that so hard to believe?"

"I—" The phone in my office rings before I have a chance to respond. Good. Since I have no idea how to respond.

"I'll start the inventory. You deal with the phone."

My mouth drops open as Sloane enters the storage room. Normally, I have to beg her to work overtime.

The phone rings again and I rush to my office to answer it.

"*Rumrunner,* this is Harper."

"Hey, Harper. It's Rhett."

I groan. Did I forget to pay the bill to *Buccaneer's Whiskey & Distillery?* Maybe if I shuffle some money around, I can find the cash needed.

"Did you get my email?"

At his question, I switch on my computer. "Summarize it for me."

"I drafted a payment plan for you at your request."

"But you said *Buccaneer's* doesn't do payment plans." When you throw your pride out of the window and ask for help, you don't forget the refusal.

"I've since discussed it with the board and we've changed our policy."

"Your board?"

There's a slight hesitation before he says, "Yes."

"Kai, the interferer, strikes again," I mutter.

"It was actually a good idea. Some of the whiskeys Jaxon is developing are higher end. More establishments will need payment plans to stock them."

I notice he didn't deny Kai was behind the change.

"I'm about done with your little brother interfering in my life."

"Can I give you some advice?"

I snort. "Something tells me you're going to dish it out whether I want it or not."

"Everyone needs help sometimes. Dakota fought me tooth and nail. She was determined to do everything on her own."

"I knew there was a reason I liked her."

"She was killing herself. There was no joy or happiness in her life. It was all work, work, work."

I bristle. "You make work sound bad."

"Nothing wrong with working hard. But it is wrong if work is all you have in your life. And now I'll shut up before you decide to beat me with your telephone."

"I can hardly beat you when we're not in the same room."

"If anyone could figure it out, you could."

He hangs up and I make my way to the storage room to help Sloane with the inventory. With her help, it takes half the time it usually does.

"I'll make up a purchase order," I say as we finish.

"I'll get the bar open."

My phone beeps with a message.

It's Carl. Just wanted to let you know all is going well. Henry had his dinner and is now watching a movie.

Thanks for letting me know.

"Is it Kai?" Sloane waggles her eyebrows at me.

"Nope. My dad's caretaker checking in."

"I didn't know you got a caretaker."

I frown. "I didn't. Kai found him."

"You should thank him." She thrusts her hips. "Without your clothes on."

"I'm not getting naked with Kai for you to win a bet."

"But naked is the best thank you."

Thank you? Should I thank Kai?

Yes, he forced a caretaker on me. And he did all the other things – found a doggy walker for Sloane, arranged a payment plan – without my consent. But they are things that have helped me.

My mother would be utterly disappointed in me for being rude to him after all he's done.

Damn. I really do need to thank him. I dig my phone out of my back pocket. What am I doing? I can't thank him with a text. My mom taught me better than this.

I guess I'm going to Mermaid Karaoke after all.

Chapter 14

"I don't need a mermaid." ~ Kai

KAI

Miles and Zane rush into my office.

"Time to go." Miles slams my computer shut.

"I was working."

Zane's head rears back. "Working? You?"

I glare at him. "I work."

Miles taps his chin as he studies me. "Do you think he's sick?"

I know I caused this myself by constantly being late, letting Jaxon do the bulk of my work, and generally goofing off during work hours. But I'm trying here. Failing to understand how to make a spreadsheet. But I'm trying.

"Piss off. I work."

"Do you think this has anything to do with Harper?" Zane asks Miles.

Harper. I can't get our kiss out of my mind. I knew the second I saw her a few months ago that it would be heaven to kiss her. And I was right. Her taste is addictive.

Too bad the stubborn woman fights me every single step of the way. It won't stop me. I know what I want and I'm not giving up. Especially since I know she wants me. She's just fighting me to fight me at this point.

"Ugh." Miles feigns throwing up. "He has the same look on his face that Rhett had when he was chasing Dakota."

"Love is in the air." Zane shivers. "No thanks."

I frown. Zane and Miles are such players. Zane always has been. But Miles was devoted to Hazel before he went off to become a professional surfer.

I'm different from them. I don't enjoy chasing women and forgetting their names in the morning. I want to be loved. I want to wake up to the same woman every morning. Go to sleep with the same woman every night. After rocking her world, of course.

"Come on." Miles flicks the lights. "We're going to Mermaid Karaoke and you're coming with."

The only reason I'm going is because the *Bootlegger* bar, where karaoke takes place, isn't far from *Rumrunner*. Maybe I can sneak over to check on Harper. Or maybe she'll come to *Bootlegger*.

Thirty minutes later, I realize I've made a mistake. *Rumrunner* is completely packed with women dressed up as mermaids and men trying to chase them. It is not my scene. When I was eighteen and sneaking into the bar, it wasn't my scene.

Miles and Zane, on the other hand, are having the time of their lives.

"What do you think of the blonde?" Miles points to a woman.

Zane's nose wrinkles. "She has trouble written all over her."

"Shall I order us some drinks?" I don't wait for their reply and make my way through the crowd to the bar.

"Alaia!" I wave to the bartender to get her attention.

"Kai Raider." She narrows her eyes at me. "Are you old enough to be in here? I need to see some ID."

I roll my eyes. Alaia was in the same class as Eli. She knows exactly how old I am.

"What are you doing slinging drinks? Are you trying to find your next story at the bar?"

"I don't exactly get to write stories for the *Smuggler's Gazette*."

The *Smuggler's Gazette* is the local free newspaper. It mostly contains help wanted ads, classifieds, and houses for sale.

"I thought the article you wrote about the sheep getting loose was funny."

She sighs. "Those Harris brothers are trouble. Speaking of trouble." She nods to the person behind me and I whirl around with a smile on my face.

"Oh." It's not Harper.

"Oh?" The woman scowls. "You're going to lose my vote for sexiest man on the island if you don't show any enthusiasm."

She reaches for me. I raise my hands in the air and back up as much as possible in this crowded bar.

"Not interested."

"If you weren't interested, you wouldn't be here."

"Kai Raider," Harper grumbles and I startle. Where did she come from? "You were supposed to go to the store to pick up baby formula and I find you in a bar two hours later?"

I shrug. "The store was out."

"And you thought the proper solution was to hit up a bar?"

"It's not my fault you can't produce enough milk for our six babies."

"Six babies?" The woman who was hitting on me rears back in disgust.

"I wasn't counting our toddlers."

"You can have him." She whirls around and stomps away.

I grin at Harper. "Thanks, Slugger."

"Once again, I didn't slug anyone."

"But you would have." I lean over to kiss her cheek. "What are you doing here? Are you here for me to remind you of what a man I am?"

She rolls her eyes. "You don't need me to remind you." She motions to the room full of women dressed up as mermaids.

I stand closer to her. "But I'm not interested in any of them." Her nose wrinkles as she contemplates me. "I'm serious, Harper. You're the only woman I see."

"I didn't come here to discuss this."

"What did you come here for? Is everything okay? Is your dad all right? Is Carl not working out?" I dig out my phone. "I have the information from the agency I found him at. They have other caretakers available. Not many men, though."

"Men?"

"I figured—"

"What?" She cups her ear. "I can't hear you."

I knock on the bar to get Alaia's attention. When she glances my way, I mimic unlocking a door. She throws me a set of keys.

I grasp Harper's hand and lead her across the room to the back, where the office is. Once we're behind closed doors, I scroll through the contacts on my phone.

"I'll reach out to the agency. I'm really sorry Carl didn't work out. He seemed competent when I did the phone interview."

Harper snatches my phone away before I can dial. "There's not a problem with Carl."

"Is it Sloane's doggy walker? I explained Boozer enjoys humping legs. She can't claim to be surprised now."

"There's not a problem with Sloane's doggy walker, but Boozer does hump a few too many legs."

"Are you mad about the payment plan? Rhett agreed it was a good idea."

She grunts. "This is exactly why I'm here."

"I promise I didn't tell Rhett anything about your money problems. He already knew you wanted a payment plan. I would never betray your trust."

"Can you stop being sweet and allow me to thank you?"

I freeze. "Thank me?"

"I'm not a heathen. I thank people when they help me out."

I smirk. "Even when you don't want them to?"

She narrows her eyes at me. "Don't push your luck."

"I'm merely pointing out how it's okay to accept help."

She grunts. I shouldn't find it adorable, but I can't help it. Harper is more prickly than jellyfish larvae in your swimsuit. But once you get past the prickly part? I've glimpsed the woman hiding beneath her stubborn, grumpy outer layer, and I'm certain she's worth it. Worth everything.

I brush her hair from her forehead. "You know. You haven't actually thanked me yet."

"It was implied."

"Come on. You can say the words. Kai, sexy demon of a man, you are the best and I thank you from the bottom of my heart."

"Sexy demon?" She grumbles but her lips are twitching.

I clutch my chest. "You don't think I'm sexy? Ouch."

"Bragging about yourself is not attractive."

"If you won't give me compliments, I need to give them to myself."

"You are beyond silly."

"But sexy silly?" I waggle my eyebrows. She chuckles. "Aha! I got you to smile."

"I smile."

I palm her cheek. "Not nearly enough, Slugger."

"Who's keeping score?"

"I am." I massage circles into her neck with my thumb and her blue eyes flare in response. I grasp her hip with my free hand and draw her near until her body collides with mine. Her breath hitches when my hard length presses against her stomach.

I can't resist her any longer. I press my lips to hers. When she sighs, I don't hesitate to thrust my tongue into her mouth. I need another taste of her. One taste wasn't enough. I will never get enough of this woman.

Harper is not a silent participant. She presses her tongue against mine until we're dueling for supremacy. I growl – I'm in charge here – and squeeze her hip. She doesn't give in. Of course, she doesn't. She's my slugger. Always ready for a fight.

I shove my thigh between her legs and she rubs herself against me for some friction.

"Is there something you need?" I ask against her mouth.

She nods. I don't force her to speak. I don't want to break the spell.

I pick her up and place her on the desk. My cock presses against my zipper. It wants out. Too bad. I'm not fucking Harper for the first time in an office in the back of a bar.

I pause with my hand on the button of her jeans. "Is this okay?"

"Yes," she hisses as she kicks off her sandals.

I snap the button open and lower the zipper. "Up," I command and she lifts her ass to allow me to draw her jeans down her legs.

I groan when her baby blue silk panties are revealed. I expected Harper to wear plain white underwear. Not sexy panties, I want to rip off of her. She continues to surprise me.

I glide my finger along the hem of her panties. Goosebumps form in my wake.

"These have to go."

She reaches for them but I stop her. "Allow me." She motions for me to get on with it.

I pull her panties down her legs. I'm tempted to get to my knees and taste her, but I don't want her first memory of me going down on her to be in an office in a bar.

"Spread your legs."

She doesn't hesitate and my cock twitches in response. I inhale a deep breath to get myself under control before parting her lips and pressing my finger against her swollen clit. She moans in response. It's all the encouragement I need.

I circle her opening with my finger while I trail kisses along her jaw. I nibble her ear and she clutches my biceps.

"Kai," she moans.

"Yes?"

"You know."

I want to make her desperate and begging for me. But I don't dare extend our time in this office any longer.

I slowly sink my finger into her. Her walls convulse around me. I add another finger and begin thrusting into her while my palm presses against her clit.

She arches into my motions. "You like that?" I growl into her ear.

"Yes," she breathes out.

"You going to come for me, Slugger?"

"That's the plan."

I smile at her grumpy response. My slugger. Even when she's in the throes of passion, she's grumpy. But not for long.

I sneak my free hand under her t-shirt to find her breast. I massage it as I continue to plunge in and out of her pussy.

Her nails dig into my biceps as she arches to meet my thrusts. Her walls tighten around me.

"Time to come, Slugger."

"I.. I…"

I pinch her nipple and she explodes. Her head drops back in a silent scream as her hips thrust up. I continue to work her until she collapses.

"Hey!" Alaia knocks on the door. "You nearly done in there? I need the computer."

Harper's head whips up and her eyes widen. "Shit. I should…"

She doesn't finish her sentence but she doesn't need to. Her regret is plain to read on her face. I sigh as I reach down to grab her jeans and panties and hand them to her.

I give her my back to allow her to dress in private. Seems strange after what we just did together, but it's what Harper needs.

The door flies open and my shoulders slump. Harper's gone.

Whereas, I want to shout from the rooftops about how wonderful she is and how much I want her, she couldn't get away from me fast enough.

So much for chipping away at the ice around her heart.

Chapter 15

"Are friends nosier than acquaintances? Answer needed urgently." ~ *Harper*

HARPER

I sprint out of the office and nearly straight into Alaia.

She puts her hands up in front of her. "Whoa!"

"Sorry. I need to…" Disappear? Learn how to perform magic and apparate? Rewind time to before I let Kai remove my jeans?

She points to the rear exit and I don't hesitate. I hurry toward it.

"You may want to button your jeans!" She hollers after me.

Great. The news of what Kai and I did in the office is going to spread around town quicker than the hurricane we had last year. Alaia is a newspaper 'reporter' who doesn't understand the difference between 'news' and 'gossip'.

At least my dad is no longer on the gossip train since he distanced himself from his friends. Although, I wouldn't put it past Jade to 'stop by' our house to give Dad the news.

I make my way from *Bootlegger* to *Rumrunner* using back alleys tourists usually avoid. Unless they're trying to find my speakeasy.

It never ceases to amaze me how the location is still secret to tourists. I figured tourists would blast the location all over social media but no one does. Or, at least, not yet.

I enter *Rumrunner* via the rear exit. It's not as busy here as it is at *Bootlegger* since Mermaid Karaoke is in full swing there. They can have their karaoke. I don't need women in seashell bras wandering around my bar bewitching the patrons.

"There you are," Sloane says when I reach the bar. "How is your dad doing?"

"Huh?"

"Didn't you go visit your dad? You didn't need to run there and back."

"Run?"

She indicates my face. "Your skin is red and blotchy, and you're sweating."

Would it be wrong to pretend I ran to check on my dad? Sloane is a native smuggler, *and* she's been betting on when Kai and I will get together. If she knew what happened in the office at *Bootlegger,* she'd tell everyone and then claim the winnings from the bet.

No thanks.

My other bartender, Dave, studies me. "You're glowing."

I rear back. "Glowing? I don't glow."

"Are you confusing glowing with glowering?" Trent asks.

I give him my Siren's Scowl. "Why aren't you at the door?"

"Told you," he mutters as he walks away. "Glowering."

The door flies open before he reaches it, and Dakota and Blossom rush inside. I hurry to them. "What's wrong?"

Dakota bends over. "Why did we run? Kai didn't say we had to run."

"Kai?"

"Oops. Was I not supposed to say his name?"

She isn't making any sense. I face Blossom. "What's happening?"

She threads her arm through mine. "We need to talk." She waves to my employees at the bar. "Harper's on break."

"I'll be back as soon as I figure out what's going on," I add.

Blossom drags me through the bar to my office with Dakota trailing behind us.

"Okay," I say once we're behind closed doors. "Why are you here?"

Blossom places a finger over her lips and tiptoes to the door. She places her ear against the door to listen. After a moment, she wrenches it open. "Aha!"

"Ah!" Sloane screams.

"Back to the bar," I order her.

"But I want to know what's happening," she pouts as she stomps away.

Blossom waits until she's gone before shutting the door and locking it. "We should be good now."

"For what?"

"No idea," Dakota says.

I turn to Blossom, who lifts her hands. "Me neither."

I rub my temples where I'm beginning to feel a headache coming on. "You must have some idea, or you wouldn't be here."

"Kai sent us," Dakota says.

"Sent you to what?"

Blossom shrugs. "All he said was to get our fine asses to *Rumrunner* because you need us."

"He didn't say fine asses," Dakota corrects.

Blossom shrugs. "It was assumed. Now, what do you need us for? I'm always up for an adventure."

Dakota groans. "Don't remind me. I am tired of the sight of blood."

"It's not my fault you're a klutz who enjoys breaking people's noses."

"I don't break noses on purpose. It just happens."

Their back and forth is not helping my headache one bit. "Do I need to get out the first aid kit?"

"Probably. With a klutzy girl around, a first aid kit is useful."

Dakota glares at Blossom. "Why are we friends again?"

"Because you love me."

"More like I'm stuck with you," Dakota mutters.

"So." Blossom rubs her hands together. "What's the adventure? Paintball at *Glowin' Galleon*? Mermaid Karaoke at *Bootlegger*? Horse riding at *Sirens & Saddles*?"

"Do not let this one on a horse. They hate her."

Blossom scowls. "Not every horse on the planet hates me."

"As much as I'm enjoying the Lucy and Ethel show, I do need to get back to work."

"Who are Lucy and Ethel?" Dakota asks.

"*I love Lucy*? A 1950s sitcom?" My parents loved watching the show when I was a kid. I've seen every episode at least four times.

Dakota shrugs. "Television wasn't part of my life growing up in care."

"I'll buy you the DVDs," Blossom says.

"And I'll what? Return to the previous millennium for a DVD player?" Dakota asks.

I blow out a breath and count to ten before I explode on them. They are ruining my post-sex high. Wait. Wait. Wait. I do not have a post-sex high. Nope. I am officially pretending what happened with Kai did not happen.

"Dakota, Blossom, do you want to explain why you're here or not? If not, I need to get back to work since I've already had a break."

"You've already had a break?" Blossom asks. "What did you do? Where did you go?"

I groan and bury my face in my hands. "Is the news all over the island already?"

"Nope. But you just confirmed our suspicions after Kai called us to come check on you."

I whip my head up. "Kai called you to come check on me?"

"Duh." Dakota rolls her eyes. "Why do you think we're here?"

"Because I was a bad mermaid in a previous life."

Blossom barks out a laugh. "Don't be silly. There are no bad mermaids."

"Yes, there are. They're called sirens, and they lead sailors to their death."

She dismisses my comment with a flick of her hand. "Sirens and mermaids are not the same species."

I'm done discussing mermaids and sirens. "Kai seriously called you to check on me?"

Blossom wiggles her phone at me. "Technically, he messaged."

"My question is, why is he worried about you?" Dakota's nose wrinkles. "Was it bad? Did he hurt you?"

"No way." Blossom shakes her head. "All the Raiders were born with the innate ability to please a woman."

My cheeks darken as I remember just how Kai pleased me. He didn't have any problems making me come in record time, unlike other men I've been with.

I don't get it. Kai is a baby. He's eight years younger than me. He was still underage when I bought this bar. How is he the man my body yearns for? It doesn't make any sense.

So much for pretending it didn't happen.

"Maybe Kai was worried her head would explode with how good it was," Dakota says and I glare at her. "What? You're not the first woman to run away after a Raider blows your mind."

"How do you know I ran away?"

"Because you're here at your bar and Kai messaged us from *Bootlegger*."

Oh, right.

Dakota pats my hand. "You don't have to tell us what happened."

"Speak for yourself," Blossom says. "I want all the details. And I also want it noted for the record that I did not run from a Raider."

"Because Jaxon ran from you before you had the chance."

I walk toward the door. "I really do need to get back to work."

Blossom sighs. "You're going to be more difficult than Dakota."

"Hey!" Dakota yells. "What did I do?"

"You worked two jobs at the same time. It's not easy to be friends with someone who's working all the time. And she," Blossom points at me, "works all the time and cares for her father when she's not working."

"This is not new information."

"No," Blossom agrees. "But now that I've decided we're going to become best friends since you'll soon be my sister, it makes things difficult."

"Sister? You are getting way ahead of yourself. Kai and I aren't dating. He's too young for me. He's immature. And he's a player. He's not the man for me."

Dakota studies me. "Who are you trying to convince? Us or you?"

Blossom pats my shoulder. "We'll start with best friends."

"Hey," Dakota says. "I'm your best friend."

Blossom shrugs. "I can have more than one."

I open the door and they walk away bickering about best friendships and sisters and I don't know what. My head is spinning from their visit.

And why did they visit? Because Kai sent them. Was he worried about me? After I ran off with my jeans around my ankles, he didn't get mad and decide I'm not worth the effort. He sent his sisters after me to make sure I'm okay.

Damnit, Kai. You're supposed to be easy to resist. You're not supposed to break through my walls. But I'm afraid breaking through my walls is exactly what he's doing.

Chapter 16

"Who knew drunken mermaids could be useful?" ~
Kai

KAI

I pause at the entrance to the alley that leads to *Rumrunner*. Maybe I should give Harper a break. After all, she ran away last night after what happened at *Bootlegger*.

My cock twitches at the reminder of how sexy Harper was when she let go. When she was in the throes of passion and forgot all her worries and her grumpiness, she was the sexiest creature I've ever encountered. More bewitching than any mermaid could ever possibly be.

I'm at the door to the speakeasy before I realize my legs have moved. Harper is impossible to resist. And I have no desire to resist her.

Trent opens the door with a smirk on his face. "I was wondering if you'd show up."

I frown. He must know what happened last night. Crap. Does the whole island know? Harper will lose what little hold she has over her temper if she finds out everyone on Smuggler's Hideaway is gossiping about her.

"You better not be giving Harper a hard time."

He snorts. "She'd have my ass in a sling if I teased her."

That's my girl. Keeping everyone in line.

"Good. She's…" I trail off when I catch sight of Harper. Trent laughs behind me but I ignore him as I make my way to her.

"Hi, Slugger. How is your day going?" I kiss her cheek in greeting.

She tucks her chin into her chest but not before I notice the blush spreading from her cheeks down her neck to her chest. My cock hardens and lengthens at memories of her flushed face when she climaxed.

"I'm fine."

I nearly chuckle at how cautious she sounds.

"How's your dad?"

Her head whips up. "My dad?"

"Did you forget you have a dad?" I tease.

"It's hard to ignore a man who snores loud enough to challenge any earplugs in existence. I don't know how Mom ever put up with him."

"Love makes you do crazy things."

"Have a lot of experience with love, do you?"

"Not yet. But I'm working on it."

I meet her gaze. Does she realize I'm referring to her? That I want to experience how it feels to love her. I started falling for her the second I laid my eyes on her.

Her eyes widen, and she retreats a few feet. Patience, I remind myself. Harper, the prickly pear, is not going to fall at my feet and declare her love after one sexual encounter. I need to wiggle my way into her life. Make myself indispensable.

"Harper!" the bartender yells.

She wrenches her gaze from mine to glance at the bartender. "What is it, Dave?"

He motions to the line of patrons waiting to be served. "Could use some help here."

"I can help," I immediately offer.

"I think you've done enough."

She doesn't give me a chance to answer before she rushes off. Why is Harper always rushing away from me? Granted, I enjoy ogling her ass as she walks. But I'd prefer her to walk toward me instead of away.

I join the line of clients waiting to be served. As I wait, I study the bar. It's a Wednesday night but it's packed in here. I don't understand how Harper can have money problems when the bar is always packed. Does she need to raise her prices?

I reach the front of the line and smile at Harper. "A Five Fathoms Summer Saison Beer, please."

She grabs a mug and pours beer into it.

"Did Blossom and Dakota stop by yesterday?"

She glares at me. "You know they did. You sent them to spy on me."

"I didn't ask them to spy. I asked them to check up on you."

"I'm a grown woman, Kai. I don't need anyone to check up on me."

I point to the overflowing beer in the mug. "It's full."

"Damnit," she mutters before flipping the tap shut. When she sets the beer down, it splashes over the sides onto her t-shirt.

"I'm not usually a klutz."

She gathers the bottom of her t-shirt and wrings out the fabric. A tantalizing amount of smooth skin is exposed. Skin, I touched yesterday. Skin, I long to touch again. And taste.

My cock presses against my zipper in a bid to get to Harper. I curl my hands on the edge of the bar before I reach for her. Before I jump over this bar and throw her over my shoulder.

She plonks the beer down on the bar in front of me and I manage to lift my gaze from her bare skin to her face.

Her brow wrinkles. "You're not making a sexual innuendo."

Because I'm afraid, if I speak, I'll drool and make a fool of myself.

"Maybe—"

"Boss!" Trent yells and cuts her off.

I spin around to face the bouncer and notice he's holding off several women dressed as mermaids.

"I got this," I tell Harper before marching toward the door.

"You don't work here," she hollers after me.

"Stay where you are," I holler back.

"Let us in." A mermaid shoves Trent. He holds up his hands and backs away.

"I think you've had enough to drink," the bouncer tells them.

"I want moonshine!" Another mermaid – this one's wearing a wet, white t-shirt over her seashell bra – shouts.

"Moonshine! Moonshine!" The other mermaids – there are five in total – begin to chant. At least, I assume they're chanting moonshine. They're slurring their words and are unsteady on their feet. Trent's right. These women have had enough to drink.

"Where are you staying?" I ask.

The first mermaid rakes her gaze over me. "Why? You wanna come with us?"

"We canna share," another one slurs.

"No, thanks. I'm not into sharing." And my balls are ready to shrivel up at the way they're looking at me. Kissy duck faces are unattractive enough but when you've had too much to drink and end up slobbering all over yourself, they're the height of unattractive.

"Where are you staying?" I repeat my question. "I can book you a ride to your hotel."

"But I don't wanna go back to the hotel," one of them screeches loud enough to make my ears want to bleed.

"There's a taxi waiting at the end of the alley," Harper whispers to me.

"All right, mermaids. It's time to go." I begin herding them out the door.

"I got this," Trent says before taking over and leading the women away.

I shut the door behind him. "I can handle the door while he deals with the women."

"Actually," Harper says but doesn't continue.

"What?"

She studies me for a long moment. I lock my limbs before I begin to squirm under her scrutiny.

"We need to talk."

Damn. I thought I was making progress with her. But I can handle whatever bullshit she throws at me to push me away. I'm not giving up.

I wasn't planning to give up before yesterday. But after yesterday? There's no way in hell I'm giving up after she allowed herself to let go in my arms.

"Okay. Lead the way."

She forces her way through the crowd until we're on the other side of the bar. She opens her office and motions me inside.

My cock twitches. It wants a repeat of what happened yesterday in another office in another bar. I inhale a deep breath to get myself back in control. Harper wants to talk. It's not time to get naked.

I settle into the chair across from her desk. "What do you want to talk about?"

She perches her ass on the desk. "You weren't hitting on those mermaids."

I rear back. "Of course not. They were drunk. They needed help, not a man leering all over them."

"And you didn't make a sexual innuendo when I lifted my shirt."

"I did not," I reaffirm since I don't know where she's going with this.

"And you didn't tell everyone what happened in the office at *Bootlegger*."

I growl. "I would never tell anyone about what we do behind closed doors. Unless you're into being watched."

"I'm not into being watched."

"Thank fuck because I don't want any other man having the privilege of witnessing your face when you come."

Her eyebrows lift. "The privilege?"

"Hell yeah, the privilege." I stand and prowl toward her. "You are beautiful, Harper Poole. The most beautiful woman on this island. Any man would be lucky and privileged to be with you."

"You don't have to flatter me anymore. I'm already going to agree to date you."

I smile. "You are?"

She holds up a hand. "But I don't share."

"Slugger, I haven't so much as looked at another woman since the first time I laid eyes on you."

She rolls her eyes. "You were eleven the first time we met."

I palm her neck. "I meant the first time I really saw you. The first time I realized what a beautiful and amazing woman you've grown up to be."

"Oh. The first time you hit me with a sexual innuendo."

I growl but I'm merely playing since she's smiling. Even her dimples have come out to play. I trace one with my finger.

"I love these dimples. I don't see them often enough."

She scowls and they disappear. "I have a busy life. I don't have time for fun."

"Wrong. You're making time for fun starting now." I kiss her nose. "I'll pick you up at eleven tomorrow for our first date."

"A date at eleven in the morning?"

"You need to work in the evening, or have you forgotten?"

"But my dad—"

I silence her with a finger on her lips. "I would never ask you to leave your dad alone. I'll ask Carl if he can come in early tomorrow."

"You've thought of everything."

She has no idea how much I've thought of her and her life. She'd go screaming straight into the ocean if she knew.

I press my lips against hers in a quick kiss. "Until tomorrow, my sweet Harper."

I leave before she can change her mind. I've managed to put another crack in the ice around her heart and I'm not giving her a chance to repair it.

Chapter 17

"Trust me. Helmet hair is an emergency." ~
Harper

HARPER

The doorbell rings and I rush to answer it.

"Slow down!" Dad yells. "It's a door, not the last call at the bar!"

I am well aware of how it's not last call at the bar since I was there for last call last night and I have the bruises under my eyes to show for it.

What was I thinking? Going out on a date with a man eight years younger than me? He's going to run away when he realizes what our age difference means as far as wrinkles are concerned.

"It's Carl," I tell him as I reach the door.

"Carl? I don't want Carl. I want a mermaid nurse with strong arms."

Carl strolls into the house. "You'll have to settle for me, old man."

"Old man?" Dad grunts. "I'm practically a spring chicken compared to you."

"Except I can use the toilet without the help of a nurse."

"Show off."

The doorbell rings again.

"What is this? Grand Central Station? Tell whoever it is to leave unless they're carrying a pizza."

I sigh. Someone's in fine form this morning.

"I don't have pizza but I can order one," Kai says when I open the door.

I cringe. "You heard Dad, did you?"

"I think the entire neighborhood did."

"Dad doesn't have volume control."

"If you leave the door open any longer, a whole flock of seagulls is going to fly in," Dad grumbles.

"Or an off button."

"Not a problem." Kai winks before strolling to my dad. "Hi, Mr. Poole."

"Mr. Poole is my father and he's dead and buried in the cemetery. If you want to speak to him, you'll have to hold a séance."

Kai chuckles. "I don't know any witches, so I guess I better stick to calling you Henry."

"Are you dating my daughter?"

If said daughter doesn't die of embarrassment before we manage to get out the door.

"I am dating your daughter," Kai answers Dad. "Assuming it's okay with you."

"Okay with me? Harper is a thirty-two-year-old woman who knows her own mind. She doesn't need my permission to date." Dad narrows his eyes. "But you better ask me for her hand in marriage before you get married."

"Dad!" I shout. "No one's getting married."

"Yet," Kai mutters.

My mouth drops open. Is he serious? He can't be serious. He must be joking. He's joking, isn't he? There's no way Kai Raider, golden boy of the Raider brothers, wants to marry me.

I stare at him. "You're skating on thin ice."

He grins. "It's a good thing I'm an excellent skater."

"You can skate? I thought you were a runner."

His blue eyes light up. "Slugger, have you been stalking me when I'm out on the trails running?"

I narrow my eyes at him. "No. I don't stalk people. Stalking is more your thing."

"Your loss. I prefer to run without a shirt on. You can ogle me all you want." He waggles his eyebrows.

"Silly me. I thought you'd advanced from the sexual innuendos."

"Not an innuendo. There was nothing indirect about my statement inviting you to ogle me."

"Are the two of you going to stand in my living room all morning?" Dad asks. "I can't hear the television over the two of you."

"The entire town of Smuggler's Rest can hear our television, Dad."

He cups his ear. "What did you say? I can't hear you."

Kai barks out a laugh and I glare at him. "Don't encourage him."

"It's not my fault your dad's hilarious."

"Hilarious?" I snort. "Yea, right." I shackle his wrist and drag him toward the door.

"My phone number is on the refrigerator," I tell Carl before I leave. "And I made you some lunch but if you don't want it, you can…" I trail off when he holds up his hand.

"I got this, Harper. Go have a good time."

I hesitate at the door. Leaving Dad with a caretaker while I work is one thing. Leaving him with a caretaker to go on a date and have fun is another. Maybe I should cancel. If Kai doesn't want to date me once Dad's arm is healed, it's his loss.

"You gonna shut that door or do you want me to pay to air condition the entire street?"

"Fine, we're leaving," I tell Dad before stomping out of the house.

Kai laughs as he leads me to his SUV.

"Don't you dare laugh at me, or we can forget all about this dating thing."

He presses me against the vehicle. "We are not forgetting about this dating thing. It's taken me months to convince you to give me a chance, I'm not giving up now."

"I won't put up with you laughing at me."

"Slugger." He brushes the hair from my forehead. "I'm not laughing at you. I wouldn't dare. You'd punch me. But your dad is hilarious."

"My dad is a pain in the ass, is what he is."

"He can be both things at once." He cups my chin. "It can't be easy for your dad. Losing your mom and then having the stroke and losing his independence."

I blow out a breath. "I know but he's a crotchety old man sometimes."

"I know. He reminds me of you." He kisses my nose and opens the door. "Now, get inside. We're going to have some fun and then eat tons of unhealthy food."

"What if I don't enjoy unhealthy food?"

He sighs. "And here I thought you were perfect."

Perfect? He can't be serious. I'm nowhere near perfect. I'm chubby despite how much physical labor operating the bar is. Plus, I'm grumpy. And I'm always exhausted.

Kai tugs on a strand of my hair. "Stop overthinking."

He slams the door before I have a chance to respond.

"You can't tell a woman to stop overthinking," I attack when he settles behind the wheel.

"Do you prefer me to list all the reasons why I think you're perfect?"

I cross my arms over my chest and fall back into the passenger seat. "I'm not perfect."

"You are to me."

"Flattery will get you nowhere."

"Is it still flattery if it's the truth?"

I don't actually know. "Where are we going?" I ask since I hate losing an argument. And, frankly, I'm afraid of how I'll react if Kai keeps saying I'm perfect.

Kai drives out of Smuggler's Rest toward Rogue's Landing.

"Are we going to steal a mascot? It's a time-honored tradition in the Raider dating book."

Each town on Smuggler's Hideaway has a live mascot. Pirate's Perch – the tiny hamlet on the other side of the island – has a foul-mouthed parrot named Plank. Smuggler's Rest has the most adorable otter known to man – Viking. And Rogue's Landing – the town in the middle of the island – has Rogue, the rambunctious raccoon.

He chuckles. "The Raider dating book? I think I lost my copy."

I guess we're not stealing a mascot. "What are we doing for our first date if we aren't stealing a mascot?"

"How do you feel about speed?"

I narrow my eyes at him. "It depends. Are we drag racing around the island? I have no intention of spending the night in jail. I have a business to operate."

He groans. "I only spent the night in jail once for drag racing and it wasn't my fault."

"Of course, it wasn't."

"We're not drag racing anyway, so you can take your lawyer off speed dial."

"What are we doing?"

"How about go-karting?"

"I don't think I've been go-karting since I was in high school."

"*Shipwreck Speedway* has improved a lot in the past few years."

"Really?" I raise an eyebrow. "No more go-karts smelling of puke?"

"Nope. And they make you wear a hairnet under your helmet."

I guess I can't complain about the foul-smelling helmets either.

Kai reaches over to squeeze my hand. "If you don't want to go go-karting, we'll go for lunch early."

I open my mouth to tell him we should go to lunch but then I notice the disappointment on his face. Damnit. I hate disappointing him. Especially after all he's done for me.

"Fine. We'll go, but at the first whiff of puke, I am out of there."

His smile lights up his face. "Deal."

He pulls into *Shipwreck Speedway* and parks in the empty lot.

"Are they open? There's no one here."

His cheeks darken. "They usually open at noon."

I glare at him. "You better not have paid someone to open early."

He lifts his hands in the air. "I wouldn't dare. You've made it perfectly obvious how you feel about my money. My buddy, Rich, works here. He said we could come in an hour early since he's here setting up anyway."

"Nice save."

He lifts my hand to kiss my knuckles before ordering me to, "Stay there."

A man who opens the door for me? You won't hear me arguing.

He opens my door and offers me his hand. "Ready to get your ass kicked?"

"It's cute you think you can beat me."

We make our way to the employee entrance, where a young kid is waiting for us. "Harper, this is my friend, Rich."

I wave in greeting and we follow him to the track.

"Whatever you're thinking, you're wrong."

"What do you mean?" I ask Kai.

"You're back to thinking I'm a child because Rich is my friend and he's only seventeen." I kind of was actually. "What you don't know is I'm Rich's big brother."

I rock to a halt. "Big brother?" He nods. "You're involved with Big Brother?"

His cheeks darken. "I know what it's like to grow up without a father. I was lucky and had five big brothers. Not everyone is as lucky."

Freaking smugglers lost at sea. Kai is not playing fair. This is supposed to be a fun date to let loose for a few hours before returning to my mundane life. This isn't supposed to be an excuse for Kai to show me there's more to him than being a goofball.

Chapter 18

"Some jokes never get old." ~ Kai

KAI

I whistle as I make my way to Eli's house carrying Mr. Crisp. Mr. Crisp is a pickle in a jar but don't let the outer appearance fool you, he's a wizard at poker. He's also my good luck charm.

Everyone is required to bring a good luck charm to the Raider monthly poker games. It all started when Miles refused to play without Hopper – his rabbit's foot that definitely isn't a rabbit. Zane complained it wasn't fair if one person had a lucky charm and the rest didn't. Miles claimed it wasn't his fault if no one else was lucky.

Somehow, it escalated into all of us being required to have lucky charms. Zane has Nugget – a taxidermized squirrel in a cowboy hat. Jaxon has a Chia Pet – the Green King – who he claims resembles Elvis but really reminds me of a green blob. Rhett has a bowling shoe because he's boring. And Eli has a set of teeth he used to scare us into brushing our teeth when we were young.

I ring the bell and grin at Paisley when she opens the door.

"How is the incubator of my future niece doing?"

"Eli!" She hollers over her shoulder. "Raider number six has arrived."

Eli comes running before I have time to enter the house. "What are you doing answering the door? You should be laying down."

Paisley fists her hands at her hips. "I should be laying down?"

"Yes." He tries to grasp her arm but she slaps at his hand.

"I am not on bed rest. I don't need to lie down."

"What's going on?" Miles asks as he and Zane join me on the porch.

"I'll tell you what's going on," Paisley sneers. "Your older brother is a control freak."

"This is not news," Zane says. Paisley hisses at him and he jumps back. "Sorry. Eli is a control freak and we should…"

"Not listen to his orders," she fills in for him.

"Agreed," Zane, Miles, and I say in unison.

"Oh no." She groans.

Eli's face pales. "What's wrong? Are you feeling contractions?" He tries to lay a hand on her swollen belly but she steps out of his reach.

"I am not feeling contractions. I'm moaning because the Three Stooges have arrived. I'll be in my lab."

"Your lab?" Eli chases after her. "You shouldn't be working."

"Eli Raider, if you tell me what I should or should not be doing one more time during this pregnancy, I'm moving back into my house."

"You sold your house."

She cocks an eyebrow. "I did?"

"What's going on?" Rhett asks as he arrives with Jaxon.

"Shush," I hiss at him. "Eli is about to explode."

"And it's going to be a big one," Miles adds.

"Does this mean I can go home?" Jaxon asks.

Rhett throws an arm around him. "There's no sense going home. Blossom is out for the evening with Dakota anyway."

I frown. "Hold on. The women are going out? Why didn't they ask Harper to join them?"

Are they excluding my woman? And make no mistake about it. Harper is my woman. We're taking it slow for her benefit, but I don't plan to ever let her go. She's it for me.

"I should have brought popcorn. I didn't realize there was a double feature tonight," Miles says.

Zane pops open a beer and hands it to him. "You keep track of the Kai drama. I've got the Eli drama."

"There is no Kai drama," I claim.

Miles points at my face. "Except you're gritting your back teeth. Goofball Kai is no longer. Welcome to Destroyer Kai."

"I'm not destroying anyone. I'm merely asking why no one asked Harper to the girls' night out."

Rhett chuckles. "As much as I'm enjoying this, the truth is, Dakota did ask Harper. She couldn't get the night off."

I frown. "She works too hard."

Rhett squeezes my shoulder. "Been there, bro. Tread cautiously."

Zane elbows me. "Unlike Eli, who apparently doesn't understand the word cautious."

"Are you serious? You didn't sell your house?" Eli asks Paisley.

"Do you have pregnancy brain? We agreed to keep my house and rent it out."

Eli's shoulders drop in relief. "There you go. You can't move back into your old house. There are renters in it."

"There are?"

"Paisley Raider," Eli growls.

Paisley holds up a hand. "We're not married yet."

"Not for lack of trying," Eli mutters.

"You're the one who wants this big, elaborate wedding. I'd be happy with a quicky wedding similar to what Jaxon and Blossom had."

"Jaxon and Blossom weren't in love when they got married."

Jaxon growls. "Watch it, bro."

Eli rests his hands on his hips. "I can't win tonight no matter what I do."

"You can hand over your poker cash now if you prefer." Zane holds out his hand.

Eli narrows his eyes at Paisley. "You waited until poker night to bring this up."

Paisley smirks. "I'm not stupid."

"I had to fall in love with a genius."

"You would be bored with anyone else."

Eli wraps his arms around her and draws her near. "I would."

"Boo!" Zane shouts as Eli dips his head to kiss Paisley. "No lovey dovey on poker night."

Paisley giggles as she retreats from Eli. "Have a fun poker night."

"Where are you going?" Eli asks as she walks past us out the door.

"I'll be back before you're finished with your game."

When Eli goes to follow her, Rhett steps in his way. "Let her go."

"She's pregnant."

"I know. The entire island of Smuggler's Hideaway knows."

Eli sighs as Paisley waves goodbye. "Fine. Come in. Let's play some poker."

Once Paisley's gone, we gather in Eli's game room. The room is exactly how you'd picture a billionaire's game room. Dark wooden paneling, green leather couches, large flat-screen televisions, a pool table in the middle of the room, and a fully stocked bar along one wall.

It's my favorite room in the house. Except for the swimming pool in the basement. You can't beat a swimming pool and sauna in the winter months when it's rainy and windy on the beach. Eli tries to keep us out. He's silly. As if we don't know how to pick a lock or crawl through a window.

"Where's your lucky charm?" Zane asks Eli.

"If you don't have your lucky charm, you automatically lose," Miles says.

"Hmmm..." Zane taps his chin as he studies our older brother. "Maybe he needs his lucky charm teeth as dentures. It happens with old men."

Eli throws a pillow at them. "I'm not an old man."

"Isn't your girlfriend older than Eli?" Jaxon asks me.

"Harper isn't my girlfriend." Yet. And I'm not discussing how Harper is older than me. It doesn't matter. End of discussion.

I rub my hands together. "Let's play some poker. Mr. Crisp and I are feeling lucky tonight."

"Mr. Crisp is a pickle. He can't feel anything," Jaxon says.

I cuddle the jar to my chest. "Don't listen to him, Mr. Crisp. He doesn't know what he's saying."

"It's an inanimate object. Inanimate objects…"

"Nope," I cut my nerdy brother off before he can give me and everyone else a lecture. Knowing him, he has a PowerPoint presentation prepared. No thanks.

Rhett places his bowling shoe on the table and pulls out a chair. "Can we just once play poker without all the goofing off and jokes?"

He sits down and *pfft*.

"Are you serious?" he asks as he jumps to his feet. "How did you even get a whoopie cushion on the chair without me noticing?"

He throws the whoopie cushion at me. "Hey. Why am I to blame?"

"Because you're a jokester who thinks fart jokes are still funny."

"Dude." Miles shakes his head. "Fart sounds are freaking hilarious."

"High five!" Zane slaps my hand.

"I have to admire how you put down the cushion without anyone noticing," Jaxon says as he fiddles with his glasses.

"Thank you." I bow.

Eli hands out glasses of whiskey before pulling out a chair. He checks there's nothing on it before sitting down and raising his glass. "To smugglers, bootleggers, rumrunners, and the mermaids who loved them."

"Smugglers!" We repeat before drinking our whiskey.

Rhett grabs the deck of cards from the middle of the table and unwraps them before shuffling and dealing. We always use a new deck to prevent cheating. As if that'll stop me.

Miles is the first one to notice something's off. He elbows Zane, whose eyes widen when he realizes the cards are special.

"I'm feeling lucky," Miles says before sliding a large stack of chips toward the center of the table.

"What did you do?" Eli asks me.

"Why me?"

"I believe it's because you are the jokester of the family."

I roll my eyes at Jaxon. "Thank you for clarifying, nerd."

"What the hell?" Rhett explodes. "These cards are marked."

He tears the first card into pieces but I jump from the table to stop him before he destroys any more. "Hey. I had to special order those."

"Does your girlfriend know you cheat at poker?"

I glare at him. "Harper isn't my girlfriend. And I didn't cheat. It was a prank."

"We discovered it in advance, it doesn't count for the prank war," Jaxon says.

"Whatever. Everyone's being boring tonight. I'm going to *Rumrunner*."

"He's running to his girlfriend because everyone's being mean to him," Miles taunts.

I ignore him. Let him think I'm upset and need comfort. If it helps me get out of here so I can spend some time with Harper, he can think what he wants.

Our date yesterday was a success but I haven't seen or heard from Harper since. She's horrible at responding to my messages. I guess I'd better go check on her.

Chapter 19

"You want to go out on a date with my Dad?" ~ Harper

HARPER

"Sorry," I greet Kai. "We can't…"

I'm cut off when his lips meet mine. "Hello, Slugger."

"Hi," I breathe out – a bit flustered by a mere meeting of our lips. This boy is trouble. And I can't seem to stop myself from wanting more. Double trouble.

"How was work last night? I tried to stop by but Miles and Zane tied me down."

I raise an eyebrow. "Tied you down?"

"Yep. Literally. Or, technically, I guess I should say they tied me to a chair."

"What did you do?"

"Nothing."

"What did you do?"

"Nothing. To them at least."

"Were you raised in a barn?" Dad yells.

"You were the one who raised me, or have you forgotten?"

"I haven't forgotten shit. Ain't nothing wrong with my brain."

"Hey, Henry," Kai greets. "How are you today?"

"I'd be a lot better if my daughter hadn't invited the entire mosquito army into the house."

I sigh and motion Kai inside. "You better come in before Dad has another stroke over me keeping the door open."

"I'll chat with your dad while you get ready to go."

"About our date." I sigh. "It's Carl's birthday. I gave him the day off."

"Not a problem."

"Yes, it is. I can't leave Dad alone."

"I'm not a child," Dad grumbles.

"Agreed. You're a grumpy old man who can't cook, dress, or go to the bathroom without help since you broke your arm."

"I got this." Kai rolls Dad's wheelchair toward him. "Hop in. Time to get dressed."

My brow wrinkles. "What are you doing?"

He motions to Dad. "I doubt he wants to go to lunch in his pajama pants."

Dad perks up. "Lunch? Where are we going?"

"Anywhere you want."

Dad gets a gleam in his eye. "The *Salty Siren* for a burger and fries?"

"I love their burgers and they have the best fries."

I glare at Dad. "You are not having a burger and fries."

"Why not? I'm a grown man. I'm tired of eating your rabbit food."

"I'm trying to keep you healthy so you can annoy the siren out of me for another thirty years."

"I'm not annoying. You're the one who complains about everything. The television is too loud, I can't sleep with your snoring."

I close my eyes and inhale a deep breath before I start to list the two million ways Dad annoys me. If I tell Dad he's annoying, he'll say I'm a complainer. And pretty soon, we'll be sniping at each other. I don't want to fight with my dad in front of Kai.

"Will one burger hurt?" Kai asks.

I growl. "Are you seriously asking me in front of my dad?"

"Duh. I want your dad to like me. I already know you like me." He winks.

"I don't know why I like you," I mutter. "You're as annoying as this one." I motion to Dad before whirling around and marching down the hallway toward my bedroom. "I'll be ready in five minutes."

When I emerge from my bedroom five minutes later, Dad is changed into a pair of jeans and a t-shirt and is waiting at the door in his wheelchair. Considering how much he hates his wheelchair, I'm beginning to wonder if Kai is a miracle worker.

"Let's go." I begin pushing Dad out of the door but Kai nudges me out of the way.

"I got this."

"But you need two people to lift the wheelchair down the stairs."

"Slugger, let me handle this."

I reluctantly step away and Kai bends at his knees before lifting the wheelchair with Dad in it and carrying it down the stairs. His muscles bulge and there's a bead of sweat on his forehead but he does it.

"You need a ramp."

"I'll get right on it as soon as my lottery winnings come in."

Kai frowns as he steers the wheelchair toward his SUV. He opens the front door and lifts Dad into his seat. I grab the wheelchair – intent on folding it and putting it in the rear – but Kai snatches it from me.

"I got it."

"I'm not helpless."

He kisses my cheek. "Nope. But it doesn't hurt to accept help once in a while."

"Whatever." I climb into the backseat behind Dad.

"Your boyfriend has a fancy vehicle."

"He's not my boyfriend."

"Why the hell not?"

"You want me to have a boyfriend?"

"I don't want you to spend the rest of your life taking care of me and not have a life of your own."

I squeeze his shoulder. "I don't mind taking care of you."

The driver's door opens and Kai positions himself behind the wheel. "Who's hungry?"

"I'm starved," Dad grumbles. "Someone keeps hiding the Fruit Loops on me."

Those bleeping Fruit Loops are going to be the death of me.

Kai chuckles. "It's a good thing we're on our way to lunch, then."

The drive to the boardwalk where the *Salty Siren* is located isn't long. Usually, we'd walk but it's a bit far to push Dad. We park and I jump out to get Dad's wheelchair but Kai beats me there.

"Let me do this for you."

"You're always doing things for me." How long will it be before he's tired of how much extra work it is to be with me?

"I enjoy doing things for you. And for your dad."

"But…"

He kisses me before I can finish my sentence. "Stop," he whispers against my mouth. "Stop worrying about everything. I'm here. I've got this."

He whips out the wheelchair and leaves me standing behind his SUV with my jaw hanging open. Does Kai – the man-child who's a goofy jokester – have this? Did he grow up and I missed it?

"Are you coming?" Dad asks. "I'm starving."

I slam the back door closed and hurry to follow them.

"Do you prefer bacon on your burger?" Kai asks Dad.

"Ain't a burger without bacon and cheese."

"What about fries? Are you a ketchup or mayonnaise with your fries person?"

"Son." Dad shakes his head. "No good man has mayonnaise with their fries. Mayonnaise is for sissies."

Kai glances behind at me and flexes his bicep. "I guess I'm eating my fries with ketchup today."

"Goofball."

"Your goofball."

I roll my eyes. "Don't try your luck, Goofy."

"Goofy's awesome. I'd be dashing in a fedora, don't you think?"

I'm afraid Kai would be dashing wearing a neon pink cropped sweatshirt and oversized sweatpants or nothing at all. Based on those muscles he was displaying earlier when he carried Dad, nothing at all has my preference.

"You gonna open the door or stare at your boyfriend with googly eyes all day?" Dad asks.

"I wasn't…" I trail off – I should know better than to argue with Dad – and hurry to open the door.

The *Salty Siren* is packed when we enter. I glance around but the only available tables are booths. Dad can't sit in a booth. Damn.

"We can go somewhere else," I suggest but I'm speaking to air.

Kai has already wheeled Dad to a table occupied by two people. "I'm sorry. Do you mind moving to the booth over there?" He points to the free booth. "We need a freestanding table for the wheelchair."

"But we already have our food," the woman complains.

Kai grabs a tray from a passing waitress and begins putting their food onto it. "Lunch is on me. Make certain to get dessert. The cherry pie is to die for."

He doesn't wait for them to respond before moving to the booth and setting their food and drinks down on the table. The woman looks at the man and he shrugs before standing and following Kai to the booth.

I remove one of the chairs and place Dad's wheelchair close to the table. Kai returns with a washcloth and cleans the table. He disappears again and this time he returns with menus.

"Did you work here?" I ask when he finally sits down next to me.

"Nah. Eli worked here when he was in high school."

"And he taught you everything you know?"

Dad scowls at me. "Stop interrogating him. He'll never want to be your boyfriend if you're always poking at him."

Kai waves a hand in dismissal. "It's okay, Henry. Harper can ask me whatever questions she wants. I'm an open book to her."

"You should be a little mysterious."

Kai chuckles. "Is that how you won your wife over?"

Dad grins. "Vikki couldn't resist me once I hit her with my charm."

Kai leans close. "Tell me more. I could use a few hints to get this one to fall for me."

"You have to leave her wanting more," Dad says.

I groan. "Please, for the love of all the pirates on the sea, do not discuss your sex life with Mom with Kai."

"A good sex life is important for a relationship. Don't you think, Kai?"

Kai raises his hands. "You're awesome, Henry, but I can't discuss what Harper and I do behind closed doors with you."

"Good."

"Were you testing me?"

"Yep. Only the best for my daughter." Dad pats my hand.

"I agree." Kai smiles at me and his blue eyes are full of warmth. And love?

No. Not love. I must be delusional. Maybe I've been reading too many romance books. There's no way Kai Raider actually loves me. We barely know each other.

Except we've known each other for years. Although, the Kai I thought I knew was a goofball jokester. I didn't expect him to be kind to my dad, arrange things like a dog sitter and a payment plan to make life easier for me or find a caretaker after Dad fell. I certainly didn't expect him to rush to the hospital to help us.

I didn't… Well, shit. I'm falling for him. Kai has somehow managed to worm his way past my walls. I pray to the smugglers he doesn't break my heart.

Chapter 20

"I'm adding mowing the lawn to my fitness routine."
~ Kai

KAI

"These are the absolute best earplugs you have?" I ask the salesperson.

She rolls her eyes. "For the hundredth time, yes."

"I want to be sure."

Harper has a hard enough life. She needs to be able to sleep when she has time. Not lie awake listening to her dad snore.

"I'll take them."

"Finally," she mutters before ringing up the purchase.

My phone rings as I'm walking out of the store.

"Hey, Zane," I answer.

"Where are you?"

"I'm on my way home from the mainland."

"Do not pass go. Do not go home. Proceed directly to *Smuggler's Cove*."

"Did we agree to have dinner tonight?"

"Miles is out. You're in."

I switch on my engine to begin the drive back to Smuggler's Hideaway. "What are you talking about?" I ask once the Bluetooth connects.

"Miles has plans. I need a wingman."

"Dude, I am not playing wingman for you."

I have no interest in spending any time at a bar or restaurant while Zane hits on women. I love my brother but he is a player. Women are interchangeable to him as long as they smell good and are pretty to look at.

"Why not?" he whines. "You were more fun before you fell for Harper."

I don't deny my feelings for Harper. It would be a lie. Besides, I don't want to deny my feelings. I want the world to know how special Harper is. How honored I am, she's with me. Even though she's still fighting it.

"You literally tied me to a chair last week at our monthly poker game because you couldn't – and I quote here – handle another prank from me."

"I need my brother."

"There are six Raider brothers. Pick another one. I'm out."

I hang up. When he rings back, I ignore it. There's no use speaking to him since he can't convince me to go out with him anyway.

I park in front of Harper's house thirty minutes later. She's not here but I don't need her for what I'm doing this afternoon.

"Thank goodness," Carl says when he opens the door. "I need to run to the store. If Henry doesn't get his Fruit Loops, he's a madman."

"I can go for you," I offer but he's already hurrying down the steps.

"The door isn't a revolving one," Henry warns. "Close it!"

"Hey, Henry," I greet when I sit down across from him.

"What are you doing here? Harper's working."

"Maybe I came to see you."

He narrows his eyes at me. "Awful early to ask for her hand in marriage. She won't acknowledge you as her boyfriend yet."

I chuckle. "The operative word being yet."

"You're a glutton for punishment, aren't you, boy?"

"Nah. I just know Harper's worth it."

"Damn straight she is."

"What are you watching?" I ask.

"Television is crap during the day. All reruns or news. Who wants to watch the news twenty-four hours a day? The world is going to the shitter. The details don't matter."

"What about a streaming service?"

"Streaming what?"

"May I?" I nod to the remote control and he hands it to me. I flip through the channels but there aren't any streaming services. I spend a few minutes hooking the television up to the streaming services I use and adding my passwords so Harper and her dad can use my accounts.

"There," I say and hand the remote control back to Henry. "You can watch pretty much anything now."

His eyes light up. "I can? Do they have any of those detective shows? Harper hates detective shows. She claims she always figures out who did it in the first five minutes, so what's the sense in finishing the show? Her mom was the same way."

I help him find some shows I think he'll enjoy. He chooses one to watch and promptly ignores me. As long as he's happy, I don't mind. Besides, I have work to do.

"I'll be mowing the lawn. Holler if you need anything."

Henry nods but I don't think he heard what I said. He's obviously fine.

I make my way to the garage and find the lawnmower. I check the gas is full before rolling the machine to the backyard and getting to work. It isn't long before I'm sweating up a storm. I remove my shirt and throw it on a table on the patio.

I finish up the backyard and switch to the front. I could use a drink, but I want to get this lawn mowed before I stop.

I mow around a tree and then aim for the next tree, only to find Harper standing in my way. I switch off the lawnmower.

"Hey, Slugger. What are you doing home?"

"Preventing a riot."

"Preventing a riot? I told your dad I would be mowing."

"Dad doesn't care since he's absorbed in some BBC police detective show only available on a streaming service."

"You can't be mad."

She raises an eyebrow. "I can't?"

"It doesn't cost me a dime to share my subscription with another household."

Her nose wrinkles. "It doesn't?"

"Nope."

"Okay. Fine."

I grin. "I think the word you're searching for is thank you."

She sighs. "Thank you."

"Thank you, manly god of my dreams."

"Don't push it. It's bad enough I had to come home from work to stop a riot."

This isn't the first time she mentioned a riot. "What are you talking about?"

She motions to the sidewalk and I glance over there to discover a row of women sitting on lawn chairs while sipping on wine.

Jade, her neighbor and my real estate agent, lifts her glass in a salute. "Best show I've seen in ages."

"I vote for him to change into shorts. I bet those legs are as muscular as his chest," Chloe – one of Paisley's good friends – says.

Jade glares at her. "You're married to a sexy cop. You don't get a vote."

"There aren't any rules about looking."

"You don't mind it when your husband ogles women on the beach?"

Chloe's nose wrinkles. "I'm not ogling."

Jade taps the corner of her mouth. "You're literally drooling."

"Drooling isn't ogling."

I return my attention to Harper. "This doesn't appear to be a riot."

She fists her hands on her hips. "And you have experience with riots, do you?"

Shit. I walked straight into that one. "It wasn't my fault. I never expected Plank to fly above the crowd making siren sounds."

"Do I want to know why Plank was free?"

"It's tradition to steal the mascots. In fact, I distinctly remember you suggesting we steal a Smuggler's Hideaway mascot on our first date."

"I did no such thing. I merely assumed we'd be stealing a mascot."

"I believe this is what your father would refer to as 'splitting hairs'."

Harper narrows her eyes at me. "I don't know if you being friends with Dad is such a good thing."

"Are you afraid I'm a bad influence on him? No need to worry. Until his arm is healed, he can't pull any pranks anyway."

She buries her face in her hands. "I've created a monster."

"A sexy monster." I motion to the women on the sidewalk. "I have proof."

"I am never going to hear the end of this, am I?"

I step closer to her and pull her hands away from her face. "Are you embarrassed by how sexy I am? Should I apologize for not having a dad bod?"

"You're not a dad, so you can't have a dad bod."

"Trust me." I wink. "It's possible."

"I need to get back to work."

"Hold on. I have something for you."

"Is this some corny pick-up line?"

I chuckle. "No, but thanks for the idea."

She groans and I release her to jog to my SUV. The women on the sidewalk clap as I pass them.

"Sorry, ladies. I'm unavailable. I only have eyes for one woman."

"I can still look," Chloe says.

"I am not messaging you the next time he mows the lawn," Jade complains.

"No worries." She points to the woman on the other side of her. "She'll message."

I grab the package with Harper's present from the front seat before jogging back to Harper. I tag her hand and lead her to the garage.

"Boo!" the women scream.

I ignore them and shut the door behind us.

"This is for you." I try to hand the bag to Harper but she holds up her hands.

"No more expensive presents."

"This isn't an expensive present," I lie. I'm betting on her never finding out how much these earplugs cost.

Her eyes narrow on the package. "What is it?"

I shove it into her hands. "Open it up and find out."

"Fine. But if it's expensive, I'm giving it back to you."

Her words are grumpy but the twinkle in her eyes gives her away. She's excited to receive a gift. How often does she receive gifts? I doubt her dad buys her birthday and Christmas presents. That shit stops now. I plan to spoil Harper.

She rips the package open. "Earplugs?"

"To help you sleep when your dad is snoring." I remove them from the box. "They're supposed to be comfortable. And they're Bluetooth enabled. You can listen to music or a podcast while you fall asleep."

"This isn't fair."

"What? You don't like them? I can return them. I kept the receipt."

She slaps me with the giftbag. "Not what I meant."

I run a hand through my hair and her gaze drops to my chest. She licks her lips and my cock twitches. It wants to feel her tongue on it. I grit my teeth before I get hard. Not the time.

"What did you mean?"

She drags her gaze from my chest back to my face. Her eyes are blazing. I groan. I can resist a lot of things. But Harper staring at me like she can't wait to touch me? I can't resist her.

I meld my lips to hers. She sighs and I thrust my tongue into her mouth. Vanilla and beer. It's a combination that shouldn't work but does. It more than works. It's addicting.

Her hands latch onto my shoulders and her fingers dig into my skin. I growl as I wrap my arms around her waist and draw her near. Her body collides with mine. I can feel the pinpoints of her breasts poking me. I draw my hand up the side of her body to the underside of her breast before—

Knock! Knock! Knock!

I wrench my lips from Harper's to glare at the door.

"Sorry, boyfriend. Just wanted to let you know the entire neighborhood can see you." Jade points to the window in the garage door.

I lean my forehead against Harper's. "How mad would you get if I bought you a new garage door?"

She bursts into laughter. It's the most beautiful sound in the world. I'd do anything to make her happy.

Chapter 21

"This day did not turn out the way I expected." ~
Harper

HARPER

I groan as I lift the keg into place. My muscles are aching, and the day is yet to begin. And it's going to be a doozy of a day.

Today is the first day of the *Moonshine & Merriment Festival*. It's basically an end of the summer party, which culminates with a dance to crown the winner of the sexiest man on the island competition.

I have no interest in the dance, but *Rumrunner* has a booth set up downtown for the festival today and tomorrow. It's a great way to earn extra cash since the festival is always packed with tourists.

And those tourists love my Mermaid Moonshine. I basically add blue food coloring and some sprinkles to Smuggler's Hideaway Moonshine and voilà – Mermaid Moonshine, the tourists can't get enough of.

Sloane runs toward the booth. "Sorry, I'm late. Boozer was throwing up all over the place this morning. I didn't want to leave him alone."

Damnit. I need Sloane today, but if her dog is sick, she can't leave him alone. "Where is he now?"

"With Pam. She's the best doggy sitter in the world."

Phew. Working the festival with two people is hard enough. With one? Practically impossible since people will riot if they can't get their drink on.

"Good. The keg is hooked up. But we need to prep the moonshine, get the…"

She holds up her hand. "This isn't my first rodeo."

We get to work. By the time nine a.m. rolls around – when we are officially allowed to serve alcohol – I'm sweaty and my back is protesting. I can't wait for Monday morning. Only forty-eight hours to go.

"Incoming smugglers," Sloane murmurs and I pop up from behind the bar to scan the area.

Kai and Zane are making their way through the crowds toward us. They aren't too hard to spot since it isn't too busy yet. Most visitors are still sleeping off their hangovers from Friday night.

"Hey, Slugger," Kai greets. When he reaches me, he tries to pull me into his arms but I step away from him.

"I'm dirty and sweaty."

Zane chuckles. "Dirty and sweaty are my favorite things."

"You would say that," Sloane mutters.

"Are you saying you don't enjoy dirty and sweaty?" He waggles his eyebrows.

Sloane rolls her eyes. "I prefer to get dirty and sweaty with someone who hasn't slept with every mermaid on the island."

Zane puffs out his chest. "Not every mermaid."

"Do you even bother to learn their names?"

I give Zane and Sloane my back. I'm not interested in their bickering. Not when Kai is standing in front of me.

"You're up early for a Saturday morning."

"I can hardly spend the day working the festival if I'm lazing around in bed."

"Working the festival? I didn't realize *Buccaneer's Whiskey* has a booth."

"We don't." He bops my nose. "But you do."

"You want to work in my booth?"

"Yep."

"Are you feeling well? Slinging drinks for eight hours under the hot sun is not my idea of a fun Saturday."

"It's a good thing you won't be slinging drinks for eight hours then."

I wipe the sweat off my forehead with the back of my hand. "What will I be doing?"

"We're here," Blossom announces as she hurries toward me. She's holding hands with an adorable little girl while Dakota trails behind her, pushing a baby stroller.

"Holy mermaids!" I squeal. "Is this Pearl and Mira?"

Dakota and Rhett are fostering the two children. There's a whole story about Dakota wanting to foster children since she grew up in care but I don't know the details since Dakota never told me and I ignore gossip as much as possible.

"This is Pearl," Blossom says, and the little girl hides behind her leg. "She's a bit shy."

Kai kneels in front of Blossom. "But she's not shy with her favorite uncle."

"Uncle Kai!" Pearl throws herself into his arms. He lifts her and flings her in the air.

"Kai," Dakota growls. "What did I say about throwing my daughter?"

Kai rests Pearl on his hip. "She loves it." Pearl giggles. She's adorable.

Kai appears comfortable with a child on his hip. As if he does this all the time. I bet he'd make a great dad. He'd be the goofy dad who the child runs to when I get mad at her.

Whoa. Hold the dolphins! I am not having children with Kai. We're barely dating. But a baby with his blue eyes would be the most adorable baby in the world.

Stop it. My hormones must be out of whack. I inhale a deep breath and get myself under control.

"Do you want to meet Mira?" Dakota asks as she lifts the baby out of the stroller.

I immediately steal the baby from her. "She's adorable, Dakota."

"She's my sister," Pearl says.

"You're very lucky to have a sister," I tell her.

Kai tickles her. "Brothers are better."

"Uh oh," Blossom says. "You're getting baby fever."

I snort. "I am not getting baby fever."

I glance over at Kai to see his reaction. *I wouldn't mind,* he mouths to me.

I ignore him. He's crazy. "Do you want to hold your niece, Zane?"

He flashes a smile but it doesn't hide the panic in his gaze. "I'm good. Mira looks happy with you. I should get going." He scrambles away as fast as he can without breaking into a run.

Dakota frowns at him. I don't blame her. An uncle should want to cuddle his niece whenever possible.

"What are you up to today?" I ask Blossom.

"We're here to pick you up."

"Pick me up?" I motion to my booth. "I'm not going anywhere."

"I'm working for you today," Kai says.

"Can I help?" Pearl asks.

He tweaks her nose. "Not this time, baby girl. But you're going to have a fun day with your mom and Blossom and Harper."

"Is Harper your girlfriend?"

"Yep."

"We're not…" I don't manage to finish my denial before Pearl asks her next inappropriate question.

"Are you going to marry her like Uncle Jaxon married Aunt Blossom?"

Kai's gaze clashes with mine. "If I can convince her."

My heart pounds in my chest. Is he seriously declaring his intention to marry me? We haven't even had sex yet. What we did at the office of *Bootlegger* doesn't count. Maybe sex with him is horrible. Maybe we're completely incompatible.

"Someone grab the baby before Harper passes out!" Blossom warns.

I glare at her. "I'm not going to pass out."

She raises her eyebrows. "Really? You're hyperventilating."

"No. I'm not."

"Well, not now since I distracted you from wedding bells."

Wedding bells? My chest spasms. She's joking, right?

Dakota lifts the baby from my arms. "She's teasing you." She glares at Blossom. "Stop it."

Blossom shrugs. "What? I want to win."

"Ignore her. Blossom thinks being competitive is a good trait. What it is, is annoying."

They must be referring to the stupid bet going around the island about Kai and me. I'm not discussing the bet. And I'm most definitely not discussing marriage or children with Kai. No way. No how.

I might be falling for the man but I'm not ready for any type of commitment. I have too much going on in my life. I want to take things slow.

Kai sets Pearl on her feet. "Have fun today, baby girl."

"Harper," Sloane hollers. "We have customers."

My eyes widen when I notice the line forming at our booth. "Coming," I start for her but Kai blocks my way.

"I'm serious. I'm working for you today."

I cross my arms over my chest. "I'm not paying you, Goofy."

"I didn't ask to get paid."

"You can't spend the entire day working the booth and not get paid."

He shrugs. "Okay. Pay me."

I growl. He knows I can't afford to pay him. I'm relying on the extra cash from the festival to pay Carl until the VA approves Dad's application for medical assistance.

He sighs before wrapping his arms around me and drawing me near. "Let me do this for you," he whispers into my hair. "I want you to have more fun. You work too hard."

I bristle. "There's nothing wrong with hard work."

"And there's nothing wrong with fun either."

"Assuming you have time for it."

"I'm giving you the time."

"Ugh. Can you stop being perfect?"

Shit. I didn't mean to say he's perfect. I blame his smell. When he's near me, I can't help but get mesmerized but his scent of whiskey and worn flannel. Like the first night you sleep in someone else's bed and realize you never want to leave.

He smirks. "I'll try, but I was born this way."

"Fine. You can spend the entire day running yourself ragged serving Mermaid Moonshine to all the visitors."

"Thank you." He presses his lips to mine in a quick, hard kiss. I lean into him for more but he lifts his head and nudges me toward Blossom and Dakota.

"Who's ready to watch a pirate fight for his woman?" I ask since I'm apparently not going back to work.

Pearl jumps up and down. "Me!"

I grasp her hand and lead her toward the main stage. Dakota and Blossom follow me.

Don't look back. Don't look back.

I glance over my shoulder. Kai waves and smiles at me.

I want to watch him wave as I leave for work every day for the rest of my life. I am falling entirely too fast for this man. Slow things down, Harper. Slow things down.

He's a child and will break my heart if I jump into a serious relationship with him. He's not ready for serious. He might think he is but he's twenty-four.

No twenty-four-year-old man wants to be serious with a thirty-two-year-old woman. Especially not a thirty-two-year-old woman with a bar to run and a Dad to care for.

Chapter 22

"Harper can knock on my door in the middle of the night whenever she wants." ~ Kai

KAI

Someone pounds on my front door and I startle awake. I scan the room. I'm in my living room on my couch with the television blaring. I must have fallen asleep while waiting for Harper to message me, she got home safe.

There's another knock on the door. I wish I could say this is an unusual occurrence but when Zane and Miles are your brothers, you never know what's going to happen.

"Coming!" I shout.

I groan as I stand to answer the door. My entire body aches from working on my feet all day at the festival. I run five miles at least five times a week. I should be able to handle a day of manual labor. I don't know how Harper does it.

"What are you…" I trail off when I open the door to find Harper on my doorstep. "Hey, Slugger."

She forces her way into my house. "You drive me crazy."

"Welcome to the club."

"You run around acting like I'm your girlfriend who you someday want to marry and have children with."

"It's not an act."

She continues to rant as if I hadn't spoken.

"You're twenty-four. I'm thirty-two. You can't possibly be ready for marriage and children. Your prefrontal cortex isn't fully formed yet."

"What's a prefrontal cortex?"

"I have no idea."

I step toward her and grasp her hands. "Then, what does it matter?"

She wrenches her hands from mine and paces the room. "Don't you get it?"

Obviously not but I know better than to say those words.

"We haven't even had sex yet! You can't run around talking about marriage and children. You don't know if we're compatible in bed."

I growl as I prowl toward her. "We are compatible in bed."

"You don't know for sure we are."

"Have we kissed?"

She rolls her eyes. "Yes."

"Did those kisses feel as if we aren't compatible?"

"A kiss isn't the same."

"Have I or have I not had my fingers deep inside you?"

A blush darkens her cheeks. "You have."

"And did I make you scream my name in ecstasy?"

"I didn't scream."

"My slugger. Always contrary."

"I'm not being contrary. I didn't scream."

"Maybe not. But you came within minutes of me touching you."

"Not fair. It's been a while since I had sex."

"Are you saying I can't make you come with my fingers within minutes again?"

Her eyes scan the room. She knows I've backed her into a corner – literally and figuratively. I place my hands on the wall to block her escape.

"Challenge accepted."

"I didn't challenge you."

"Harper, you did and you know it. You came here ranting about not having had sex with me yet."

"I didn't lie."

I brush her hair from her forehead. "Make no mistake about it. I want to have sex with you. I've been trying to take things slow."

"We should take things slow."

My cock deflates. It's ready to bury itself deep inside her right here, right now but if she isn't ready, it'll have to wait. I step back and drop my hands.

"Okay, Slugger. We'll take things slow."

"Seriously?" She narrows her eyes at me. "You're going to give up? Just like that?"

I growl. "I'm not giving up. I will never give up on you. I'm giving you what you want."

"I don't want you to regret being with me."

"Regret being with you? I could never regret having sex with you."

She rolls her eyes. "Easily said."

I slam my hands against the wall. "No, it's not easy. Do you have any clue how fucking hard I am right now? Just because you're here and I can smell you. Or how about how I lay in bed every night and replay what we did in the office at *Bootlegger* with my cock in my hand."

Her eyes flare. "You do?"

"You're the sexiest woman I've ever known. The moment I laid eyes on you several months ago, I was a goner."

I shut up before I confess my love to her. I don't love her. Not yet. But I'm pretty fucking close.

"I came here to seduce you."

My cock pulses against my zipper at her confession. It urges me to strip her. To shove it deep inside her.

I inhale a deep breath. If Harper and I are finally having sex, it won't be fast and furious. Not if I can help it.

"And now? Do you still want to seduce me?"

"I suck at seduction."

"You're not doing a bad job." I press my hard length against her stomach and she gasps.

"This is ridiculous. I read enough romance books. I should know how to seduce a man. Maybe I should stop reading paranormal romances. The werewolf takes one look at a woman and knows she's his mate. And boom! They're banging. And the Hallmark movies always end with a kiss. There's no seduction happening. I can't learn from them."

I tuck a strand of hair behind her ear. "I always knew you were a secret romantic."

"You did not."

"You bought a fancy bottle of champagne for Blossom and Jaxon when they announced their love for each other."

She sighs. "I'm happy for them."

"Romantic."

She glares at me. "You better not tell anyone I'm a romantic."

"I won't tell anyone anything. Not how you're a romantic." I kiss her neck and she tilts to offer me better access. "Not how you drive me crazy." I nibble her ear. "Not how you scream for me when you come."

She grasps my t-shirt. "Make me scream, Kai."

"Are you sure?"

She nods.

"Say the words, Slugger."

"I'm sure."

"I'm sure I want you, sexy demon, to make me scream."

She barks out a laugh. "Sexy demon?"

"I guess I need to prove to you what a sexy demon I am." I throw her over my shoulder.

"Eek!" she squeals.

I slap her ass. "Stay steady or I'll drop you."

"Don't you dare drop me."

I enter my bedroom and throw her on the bed. I whip off my t-shirt before crawling onto the bed between her legs.

I fiddle with the hem of her t-shirt. "May I remove this?"

"Are you going to ask my permission every step of the way?"

I kiss her stomach. "I don't want you to have any regrets."

She smiles at me and her dimples come out to play. "I won't have any regrets, Goofy."

"And you won't think I'm goofy after tonight either."

"Promises. Promises."

"Arms up." She lifts her arms and I yank her shirt off, leaving her in a white lace bra. "This is one sexy bra, Slugger."

"I didn't wear it for you. I wore it for me. It makes me feel pretty."

"I can't wait to see what other sexy lingerie you have."

"If you're going to stare at me all night and not touch me, you won't get a chance."

"I'll touch. Don't you worry." I grin. "Hands on the headboard."

She hesitates for a moment before reaching above her to clasp the headboard. "Good girl," I mutter before drawing my fingers up her sides to reach her bra. "This is pretty but it has to go. I want to see your breasts."

I flick the front clasp open and shove the material out of my way. I trace her nipple with my finger and watch as goosebumps form. I love how her body responds to me.

I bend over and latch onto her nipple. She moans and arches her back to push her breast into my mouth. I toy with her nipple. I lick and nibble until it's a hard point. Then, I switch to her other breast.

Harper wraps her legs around my waist and grinds her core against my cock. I can feel how hot she is through her jeans.

"If you want this to last, you need to stop grinding against me."

"I want you to make me scream."

Which is what I'm doing. I want to drive her wild with need. Until she can't help but beg for my cock. I want to hear my pretty woman beg for me. I want her dripping with need for me.

I lick her nipple before blowing on it and she moans as her legs tighten around me. My cock presses against my zipper. I'm going to have an imprint of my zipper on my cock before the night is done. Worth it.

"Please," Harper breathes out.

"What do you need?"

"You. In me."

"But I'm not done playing with these pretty nipples." I tweak one and she swears under her breath.

"You're cruel."

I fiddle with the snap of her jeans. "Is it cruel if I remove your jeans?"

She releases the headboard and slaps my hand out of the way. I shackle her wrist. "Hands back on the headboard."

"But you're taking forever," she whines.

"Do you want me to make you come?" She nods. "Do you want me to make you scream?"

"Yes, please."

"Put your hands back on the headboard."

She hurries to follow my order. I duck my chin to hide my amusement. If she thinks I'm laughing at her, Grumpy Harper will make an appearance and shut things down.

I snap open her jeans and draw the zipper down, revealing her white lace panties. I want to rip them off but I stop myself. Harper worked hard to pay for these. I can't wait to buy her sexy panties I can rip off.

I shove her jeans and panties down her legs in one go. I pause to appreciate the moment. Harper is finally in my bed. Naked and wanting me. It's a dream come true.

"If I'm naked, you should be too."

I don't hesitate. I remove my jeans. My cock springs out, aiming straight for Harper. Her eyes flare and I tug on it a few times. She rubs her legs together in response.

I tap her foot. "Spread."

She widens her legs and I kneel between them. I reach across her to open my nightstand drawer for a condom. I yank and the entire drawer opens before falling to the floor.

Harper giggles at my overenthusiasm. She can laugh all she wants. I'll have her moaning soon. And screaming later.

I don a condom and brace myself over Harper with my cock notched at her entrance.

"There's no going back from this, Harper. Once I've had you, I'm not letting you go."

I meld my lips to hers before she can respond. I don't want to argue with her. Not here. Not now.

I tease her opening with my cock while I memorize the taste of her mouth. The feel of her breasts pushing against mine.

I inch inside and moan at the feel of how hot and wet she is for me. I want to tease her more, but I can't resist sinking into her until my balls slap against her ass.

She feels better than anything I've ever experienced before. She feels like home. Like forever.

Fuck, not being in love with this woman. I was lying to myself before when I said I wasn't there yet. I'm there. I love her. And I'm going to convince her to fall in love with me.

Starting with getting her addicted to my cock.

Chapter 23

"Seriously. I don't beg." ~ Harper

HARPER

I cuddle into the warmth behind me, and it moans.

Moans? How does warmth moan?

I force my eyes open and scan the room. Wait a smuggler's minute. This isn't my room.

The memories come flooding back. Knocking on Kai's door in the middle of the night. Practically begging him for sex.

I wanted it to be romantic. I did not achieve my goal.

But the sex. Holy mermaids flirting with pirates on the sea! It was hot and satisfying and made my toes curl. I may have even screamed in pleasure. I won't be admitting that to Kai, though.

My gaze lands on the clock. Eight a.m.

"Smugglers!" I screech and try to sit up. Kai's arm holds me down. "Let me go."

"Not a chance. I warned you, if we had sex, I wouldn't let you go."

I slap at his hand curled into my side. "We can discuss our relationship status later. I need to go."

"Where do you need to go?"

"Kai, if you don't move your hand, I'm going to remove your balls with the dull, rusty knife we use to cut lemons at the bar."

He snatches his arm away. "You have a scary imagination."

I jump out of bed and my breasts bounce with the motion. I'm naked. How did I forget I'm naked? Did Kai perform some kind of sex magic on me last night?

"Where are my clothes?"

"Calm down, Slugger."

"You did not just tell me to calm down. I knew it." I shake my head. "This was a mistake."

He growls before launching himself out of bed and prowling toward me. "You promised me you wouldn't think this is a mistake."

I throw my arms into the air. "I also didn't expect to fall asleep and forget all about my dad. He's probably lying in a pool of his piss now." I groan. "I really don't want to clean up piss this morning. At least the *Moonshine & Merriment Festival* doesn't kick off until noon today."

Kai shackles my wrists. "Slugger."

I yank my hands away but his grip is too strong. "Let me go, Goofy. I have to get home."

"I already phoned and checked on your dad."

My brow wrinkles. "Dad answered the phone? He never answers the phone. He claims there isn't anyone he wants to speak to unless Mom is reaching out from beyond the grave."

"I spoke to Carl."

"Carl? Carl the caretaker? He should have gone home by now."

"When you fell asleep last night, I rang him and asked him to stay over."

"You did what?" This time, I'm strong enough to yank my hands away. "Carl doesn't work for you. He works for me."

"This is why I tried to wake you. I knew you'd go full on Mermaid frenzy on me."

"Hold on. You tried to wake me?"

"I'll be honest. I didn't want to. I wanted to sleep next to you all night long."

He wanted to sleep next to me all night long? And here I was worried he would chase me away once he got into my pants. Maybe Kai is more mature than I give him credit for.

"I didn't get here until three in the morning. All night long wasn't possible."

"Nonetheless. I didn't want you to leave. I tried to wake you since I knew you'd want to get back to your dad. But you were out cold."

"I was out cold?" I don't believe him. I'm not a sound sleeper.

"Yep. I took a selfie as proof."

"Kai Raider. If you took a naked selfie of me, I'm going to throw you to the sirens without any clothes on."

He smirks. "Sounds like fun."

I glare at him. "And I'll phone your mother and tell her what you did."

"You play dirty." He picks up his phone from the nightstand and hands it to me.

"What am I supposed to do with this?"

"Look at the picture so I don't have to answer to my mother why I have a girlfriend she hasn't met yet."

I freeze. "Hasn't met yet? You want me to meet your mother?"

"Duh. You're my girlfriend. You're not getting rid of me. Of course, I want you to meet my mother. I'd say meet my family but you already know my brothers."

I've never met the mother of a boyfriend before. Probably because I haven't been in a relationship that lasted more than a few hookups. It's hard to find love when you work sixty hours a week and care for your father during every free moment.

I can't deal with this now. One thing at a time.

"Show me the picture." I try to hand the phone back to him.

"The code is 1101."

"1101 isn't a very secure code."

He shrugs. "It's the day I first saw you."

Kai being sweet and romantic is another thing I absolutely cannot deal with now. I tap the security code and open his gallery. Sure enough, there's a selfie of us. There's a sign with 'I fell asleep' written on it on top of me, while Kai makes a crazy face next to me.

"You made a sign?"

He shrugs. "I figure our kids will get a kick out of the picture someday."

The list of things I don't want to deal with is piling up. Kids someday?

"Your clothes are folded on the chair." He points to the corner. "The bathroom is behind the door next to the chair. I'll go make you some coffee and put it in a travel mug."

"Make me coffee in a travel mug? Are you trying to get rid of me?" What is going on here? I've obviously been out of the dating scene too long. This is confusing me.

"Harper. Harper." Kai taps my chin and I blink my eyes until I can focus on him. "I'm not trying to get rid of you."

"Coffee in a travel mug doesn't say: Welcome. Stay for a while. I'll make you some breakfast before I rock your world again."

His eyes flare and he steps close. Since we're still naked – why are we still naked!? – I can feel his dick hard and heavy pressing against my stomach.

"Harper Poole, my little slugger, I would love to make you breakfast before rocking your world again."

"But you're making me coffee in a travel mug instead."

He palms my neck. "You are obviously freaking out. I don't want to push you. I want to give you space to calm your mind."

This is why I'm falling for him. He gets me. I don't know how or why, but Kai Raider understands me. This man, who is eight years younger than me understands me better than any man my own age I've dated.

I need to stop using his age as an excuse. He's not the same kid I thought he was months ago. A kid wouldn't have found help for my dad, mowed my lawn, insisted on working at my booth at the festival to give me a day off or done any of the other wonderfully insightful things he's done for me without asking.

I'm definitely falling in love with him.

"Thank you."

"You're welcome." He kisses my cheek before strolling for the door.

"Aren't you going to get dressed?"

"And miss you drooling over my body?"

"I'm not drooling over your body."

"And you didn't beg me to let you touch me last night either."

"I didn't beg."

He smirks. "Sure, you didn't."

My stomach rumbles and he frowns. "When was the last time you ate?"

I scrunch up my nose as I try to remember. "I had a bunch of junk food with Blossom and Dakota, but I think I skipped dinner. It was packed at *Rumrunner* last night. Trent had to turn customers away when we reached capacity."

"I should have helped."

"Um, you did help. You worked the booth all day. You can't work the booth all day and then work the bar until closing."

"Who says?"

My stomach rumbles again and I place a hand over it in an effort to quiet the traitorous organ down.

"Do you want a breakfast sandwich to go or pancakes?"

I'm confused. "What?"

"Not a pancake lover? I can make eggs and sausage."

"You can cook?"

"All of the Raider brothers can cook. Mom was too busy working after Dad fucked off. Everyone pitched in to help."

"I'm sorry."

"It's done and dusted. Nothing to be sorry about."

I disagree but I don't get a chance to question him before he speaks again.

"What do you want for breakfast, Slugger?"

"Eggs and sausage."

"Go. Get dressed. I'll have your breakfast ready in a few minutes."

"You don't have to take care of me all the time."

He smiles. "It's my privilege to take care of you."

I wait until he leaves before collapsing on the bed. How am I going to resist this man if he continues to be this sweet? The heroes of my romance books don't have anything on Kai Raider.

And – spoiler alert! – I did not resist him last night. Or any of the other times he's kissed me or touched me.

Chapter 24

"I blame the fork." ~ Kai

KAI

Harper answers her door and frowns at me. "What are you doing here?"

I press my lips to hers and kiss the frown off her face. "I think the words you're searching for are. Hello, sexy demon, how are you this morning?"

She snorts. "Sexy demon?"

I step closer and lower my voice. "Do I need to demonstrate again how much of a sexy demon I am?"

Her eyes flare and she bites her lower lip. "Maybe?"

I groan. "You are a temptress, Slugger. But the sexy times will have to wait. We're expected at Mom's house in fifteen minutes."

"We were going to meet you there."

"You're cute." I tweak her nose before pushing past her into the house. "Henry, my man, are you ready to eat your weight in potato salad with a side of hamburger and hot dogs?"

He perks up. "Let's go."

I chuckle as I roll his wheelchair over to him. "Hop in. Your chariot awaits."

"Hold on," Harper says. "I told you we can meet you at the barbecue."

"Why would we do a fool thing like that?" Henry asks. "Your boyfriend has a nice big SUV and he can carry me down the porch steps instead of trying to kill me by dragging me down them."

Harper growls. "If I was trying to kill you, you'd be dead, old man."

"Involuntary manslaughter then."

Harper groans. "You and those BBC detective shows."

I help Henry into the wheelchair. "Which one is your favorite?"

"There's one set during the war and the detective solves murders on the home front in England."

"Sounds interesting."

We reach the top of the steps on the porch and Harper rushes to us. "Let me help you."

"You can help by ogling my muscles as I carry your dad down the stairs."

"I don't ogle."

"Sure, you don't." I wink before lifting the wheelchair and carrying it down the stairs. It's not an easy task, but it's better than letting Harper help. I don't want her hurting herself.

"Why don't you have a ramp?" I ask once I'm driving toward Mom's house.

"They're expensive. I tried to get a subsidy but it wasn't approved."

I frown. A subsidy should have been approved. How is Harper supposed to get her dad up and down those stairs without a ramp?

We arrive at the ranch house where Mom and my step-dad, Stuart, live five minutes later. They live a little out of the town of Smuggler's Rest. Mom said after raising six boys, she needed some peace and quiet.

"Is this the house you grew up in?" Harper asks as I push her dad toward the back yard.

I shake my head. "Eli bought Mom this house when he earned his second million."

"What did he do with his first million?"

"He took all of us on this exclusive beach vacation for two weeks."

"Holy mermaids," she whispers when we reach the back yard.

It's a pretty cool area. There's a pool with a slide and hot tub attached, a fire pit where we hold competitions for best s'more, a lounge area with a television to watch games on, and an outdoor kitchen with a barbecue, refrigerator, and outdoor stove.

Mom spots me and she elbows Stuart, who's manning the grill. He captures her hand and they make their way to us.

I kiss Mom's cheek. "Mom, Stuart, this is Harper and her dad, Henry."

"Thank you for inviting us," Harper says. "I'm sorry I'm arriving empty handed – I do know better – but Kai insisted you had everything covered."

"You'll thank me later. She wanted to bring homemade coleslaw."

She elbows me. "You did not just tell your mom, who I met three seconds ago I'm an awful cook."

"It's not a lie," Henry says. "She can ruin a peanut butter and jelly sandwich."

Harper fists her hands on her hips. "I guess you'll be making your own food from now on. Oh wait. You can't because you broke your arm being foolish."

"It's not foolish to not want to be a burden."

"Dad, you're not a burden."

"Which is why you have your first boyfriend at the age of thirty-two."

Harper's cheeks darken as she glares at her dad. "Kai is not my first boyfriend."

"First one I've met."

I throw my arm around her shoulders. "At least you're admitting I'm your boyfriend."

"You're not…" She blows out a breath. "Whatever."

Mom smiles at us. "I'm happy for you, Kai. I admit I was a bit worried when I found out my baby boy is dating a woman eight years his senior, but you two are perfect for each other."

"I've been trying to tell her as much for months but she wouldn't give me a chance until recently."

Mom nods in approval at Harper. "Good. Things come too easily to Kai. He needs a woman who challenges him."

"If everyone is done approving my daughter, who is a pain in my ass but deserves the best in life, I'm hungry."

Harper rolls her eyes at her dad. "Of course, you are."

She starts pushing him toward the tables and chairs set up next to the outdoor kitchen, but Stuart nudges her out of the way.

"I've got this. Henry and I will get better acquainted."

"As long as acquainted comes with potato salad and a hamburger, I'm in."

Zane saunters toward us. "Did someone say potato salad?"

"Zane, this is my dad, Henry," Harper introduces. "Dad, this is one of Kai's brothers. He has five."

Henry's eyes widen. "Six children? All boys? I could barely handle one daughter."

"Dad," Harper grumbles. "I was a perfectly pleasant daughter."

He points at her with his broken arm. "The police brought you home after you got caught sneaking out of *Rumrunner*."

Zane rubs his hands together. "Excellent. Henry can tell us all about Harper when she was young. I need some blackmail material for the next time she cuts off my drinking at the bar."

Harper glares at him. "If I cut you off, I cut you off."

"I thought your employees were kidding about the Siren's Scowl. They were not." Zane shivers.

"No giving my daughter a hard time at the bar," Henry orders.

"Welp. We know where Harper got her grump from," Zane mutters before wandering away.

"Being grumpy isn't hereditary," she hollers after him but he ignores her.

"I was promised potato salad and a burger," Henry says and I bark out a laugh.

We make our way to the tables and chairs where the rest of the family is gathered. Pearl notices me and rushes my way.

"Uncle Kai!"

I pick her up and throw her in the air. She giggles, and Harper's eyes soften.

Pearl points at Henry. "Who is he? Why is he in a chair?"

I set her on her feet and Harper takes her hand. "This is my dad, Henry. Dad, this is Pearl. She belongs to Rhett and Dakota."

"Why are you in a chair? Can't you walk?"

Dakota gasps and rushes over. "We don't ask those sorts of questions."

Pearl's nose wrinkles. "Why not?"

When Dakota appears to be at a loss, Harper steps in. "Because sometimes the reason why someone is in a chair or can't walk is very sad and makes them sad."

Pearl's bottom lip trembles. "I don't want to make anyone sad."

Harper squeezes her hand. "It's okay. You didn't make my dad sad. He's a grump. He doesn't get sad."

"I'm not the only grump," Henry grumbles and Harper glares at him. "What? Kai's brother said it. Not me."

"Dad, don't make me throw you down the porch stairs."

I chuckle and Harper switches her glare to me. I lift my hands. "Sorry."

"Do you want a ride in the wheelchair?" I ask Pearl.

Her eyes light with excitement. "Can I?"

I situate Henry in a chair at the head of the table before wheeling the chair toward Pearl. "Hop on."

Rhett stands. "Out of my way. You are not pushing my daughter around in a wheelchair."

Pearl tugs on his jeans. "Don't be a grump, Daddy."

"Do you remember the time he pushed you around the house in my office chair? You had to get stitches."

"It was one stitch. One," I argue but I move out of the way so he can give Pearl a ride with Henry's wheelchair.

I grab two plates and fill them with food. I tuck two beers under my arm before nudging Harper. "Come with me."

"Where are we going?" she asks but she doesn't hesitate to follow me.

"There." I nod toward a set of Adirondack chairs at the end of the yard.

She sits and I hand her the plate of food and a beer before settling in the chair next to her.

"Wow. The view of the ocean is amazing from here."

"It's the reason Mom wanted to build on this land."

"Your mom is a smart lady."

"Stuart built this seating area for Mom. He proposed to her here."

"Why is there a growl in your voice?"

"Sorry." I clear my throat. "Stuart messed up when he first started dating Mom. She forgave him, so I did as well but I haven't forgotten."

"It must be difficult. I can't imagine how I'd feel if Dad started dating again. He loved Mom so much."

"My dad wasn't as devoted to my mom. He left her with six kids and started a new family somewhere else."

She squeezes my hand. "I'm sorry."

I shrug it off. "I was ten when he left. I'm over it."

"I was fourteen when Mom died. I'm not over it."

"Sorry, I—"

"I'm not begging for sympathy. I'm just trying to say I understand how the loss of a parent at a young age can affect your whole life."

"Losing Dad hasn't affected my whole life."

She smiles at me and I can't resist those lips. I lean over the armrest and meld my mouth to hers. The armrest digs into my waist but Harper is worth a little pain. She's worth everything. She's my everything.

If she left me the way Dad left Mom, I'd be devastated. I wouldn't be able to go on. I wouldn't want to find another woman to love and marry. Never.

The thought of losing her has me grunting and Harper pulls away. "What's wrong?"

"I poked myself with my fork." It's not a lie, although it's not why I grunted.

"We should probably eat before the rest of your cutlery joins the fork."

We relax back in our chairs. Harper stares at the ocean as we eat, but I can't keep my eyes off her.

"Do you want to stay living in town or would you enjoy a place similar to this?" I motion to the ocean.

"This is lovely, but I can't imagine ever leaving the house I grew up in. Although, a pool would be awesome. Dad did aquatic therapy after his stroke and now he loves to swim but navigating the sand to get to the ocean is too difficult."

"You can use Mom's pool whenever you want."

She raises an eyebrow. "Shouldn't you ask your mom first?"

"Nope. You're family now. You don't need to ask."

Her breath hitches. "I'm not family, Goofy."

"What do you think of this beer?" I ask since I don't want to argue with her. But she is family. She's just not ready to hear those words yet.

I understand. She's been alone with her dad for a long time. She's not used to having a big, rambunctious family.

What she doesn't realize is, a big family means there are more people to share the load. I'm honored to be the person to introduce her to how wonderful having a family means.

Chapter 25

"But I wanted a marshmallow." ~ Harper

HARPER

"Why are you nervous?" Kai asks.

"I'm not nervous," I lie.

"Okay. You're not nervous. Why are you dressed in black?"

"I always dress in black."

"No, you usually dress in a black t-shirt from *Rumrunner* and a pair of jeans. You're wearing black pants."

"When did you become Mr. Observant?"

He squeezes my thigh. "When it comes to you, I'm always observant."

"Sure you are, Goofy."

"Why did you insist on driving your car?"

"Are you going to question me all night?"

"Yes." He nods. "Until you tell me what we're doing for our date."

"What if I want to surprise you?"

"Surprise me how? If you want to have sex on the beach, I'm in." He wiggles his eyebrows.

My nose wrinkles. "The sand gets everywhere. And I do mean everywhere."

"Okay. No sex on the beach. What else requires you to wear dark clothes?" He taps his chin. "Pranks obviously require dark clothes."

I gasp. He wasn't supposed to figure out what we're doing until we arrive. I probably should have skipped on the black beanie.

"Harper Poole, are we performing a prank?"

I shrug. "Maybe."

"I hope it's better than Blossom's idea for a prank."

"What if it's not?"

"I don't care. I was joking. I'm excited you're up for trying new things. Maybe later we can try new things in bed."

My nipples tingle at his suggestion. I'm ready for another night spent in Kai's arms. But he needs to make the first move. We only had sex the last time because I attacked him the night of the *Moonshine & Merriment Festival.*

"What kind of new things?"

He traces a finger down my arm. "How do you feel about handcuffs? Or what about a mask?"

His suggestions, combined with his gravelly voice, have me squirming in my seat. It's a good thing we're nearly at our destination or I'd park near a deserted dune and have my wicked way with him. So much for Kai making the first move.

I clear my throat. "We're here."

He looks around. "Why are we parking in the center of Rogue's Landing?"

"We can't exactly steal Rogue the raccoon if we're not in Rogue's Landing."

His jaw drops open. "You want to steal Rogue?"

"Rogue hasn't been successfully stolen since I was in high school. What better way is there for you to win the prank war with your brothers?"

"What do you know about the prank war?"

I turn to face him. "I know you're losing."

He bristles. "I am not losing." I raise an eyebrow. "I'm not winning but I'm not at the bottom, losing either. Jaxon is always at the bottom."

"Your brothers told me all about the prank war at the barbecue last week."

He sighs. "I knew they were up to something when they kidnapped you."

"They didn't kidnap me."

"They carried you away from me."

I tap his nose. "No pouting or I won't let you come with me to steal Rogue."

His eyes light up. "What's your plan?"

I hold up a bag of marshmallows. "Rogue loves these. We'll lure him to us with marshmallows and then we'll escape with him. Easy peasy."

Kai laughs. "Let's do this."

We exit the car and he captures my hand. "Do you know where Rogue is or are we going to walk around town offering marshmallows to everyone?"

"Of course, I know where Rogue is. I own the most popular bar on Smuggler's Hideaway. I know everything happening on this island."

He freezes. "You do?"

I bite my tongue to stop my smirk. "Why? Is there something about you, you don't want me to know?"

He groans. "You know, don't you?"

"Know about the time you went running through a field of sheep without any clothes on?"

"I had shoes on."

"Or about the time you got kicked out of *Bootlegger* for starting a game of The Floor is Lava?"

"No one got hurt. I don't care what Alaia says."

"Didn't you end up with eight stitches and a concussion?"

"It was only six stitches," he mutters.

I giggle. "Oh, in that case."

Kai dives after me and tickles my ribs. "Are you laughing at me, Slugger?"

I try to bat his hands away. "Stop! Stop!"

"What will you give me if I stop?"

I hold up the bag of marshmallows. "You can have a pink one."

He reaches for the bag but I hide it behind my back. "After we capture Rogue."

He motions me forward. "Let's go."

We begin walking again and Kai captures my hand. He squeezes it and smiles at me. My heart thumps in my chest. I want to see his smile every day for the rest of my life.

Whoa, Harper! Don't get ahead of yourself. Kai is young. He has lots of exploring to do before he settles down with someone more age appropriate. Assuming the goofball ever settles down.

"Here we are." I motion to the alleyway running between two rows of houses. "It should be the third house on the left."

We reach the gate in the wooden fence. I unlatch it and start to open the gate but Kai stops me.

"Let me go first. In case, anyone's home."

"No one's home. Norm has bowling tonight. And Amy is at book club."

His mouth drops open. "You seriously know everything happening on this island."

"Told you so."

We enter the backyard and I make a beeline for their shed. "They keep Rogue in here when they're gone." I pull on the door but it doesn't budge. "Crap on a smuggler. It's locked."

Kai nudges me out of the way. "No problem." He fiddles with the lock for a minute before grinning at me and opening the door.

"Remind me to add a security chain to my front door."

He frowns. "I wouldn't break into your house."

"Maybe not but you have five brothers."

"I'll buy a security chain at the hardware store tomorrow."

Something in the dark hisses and I switch on the light. "Hey, Rogue," I greet the hissing animal. "I brought you marshmallows."

Rogue immediately stops hissing and sticks his paw through the cage. I place a marshmallow in it and he skitters to the corner of his cage with his prize.

Kai picks up the cage. Rogue briefly looks up but isn't bothered by this development. "Lead the way."

I hurry out of the shed and to the gate. I open it and run into the alleyway. I trip and fly through the air before hitting the ground with a thump.

"Ow!" I push my hair out of my face and notice Sammy the seal lounging in the alleyway. In my rush, I didn't see him.

"Sammy, what are you doing in the alleyway?"

Sammy is a Smuggler's Hideaway legend. The seal was released from a Marine Sanctuary to the north of the island. When he arrived here, he realized he didn't have any interest in frolicking in the sea.

He decided to stay on land and become a complete menace to the locals. He's lucky he's cute or between blocking traffic and invading people's homes, he never would have survived this long.

"Harper." Kai rushes to me. He sets Rogue in his cage down next to Sammy. "Are you hurt?"

"I think I bruised my elbow."

He frowns. "You're bleeding."

I point to the seal. "It's Sammy's fault."

Sammy honks in response. "Don't honk at me. I'm not the one blocking the alleyway." He barks and I wag a finger at him. "Being cute doesn't mean you can hang out wherever you want."

Rogue snarls and hisses at Sammy and Sammy growls in return.

"Shit. Where are my marshmallows? We need to quiet Rogue down before he alerts the entire neighborhood."

"You're not seriously thinking of stealing Rogue now?" Kai asks.

"What do you mean? It's not as if Sammy will tell on us."

"You're bleeding, Harper."

I roll my eyes. "This isn't bleeding. I've bled more from a broken bottle cap."

He scowls. "I'm serious, Slugger. We need to get your elbow checked out."

"I'm fine. You're acting weird. Are you sure you're not the one who fell?" I get to my knees and he helps me to my feet.

"What's all the racket?" a man yells before he opens the gate to the alleyway. He notices the cage. "Are you stealing Rogue?"

"Who's stealing Rogue?" another man yells before he enters the alleyway with a woman.

"I'm phoning the police," the woman says.

"Let's go." Kai pushes me toward the road but I plant my feet.

"We need to get Rogue first."

"They're going to call the police."

"But if we ditch Rogue, we've failed."

He cups my face. "Slugger, I don't give a shit if the prank failed. You tried. You let loose. Witnessing you have fun when you usually don't have time for fun is the biggest privilege of my life."

I blink up at him. "Are you sure you didn't hit your head?"

He kisses my nose. "There's more to me than the goofy guy."

"The police are on their way," the woman shouts.

Kai shackles my wrist and drags me away from the crowd. "If you get arrested, your dad will tan my ass."

I roll my eyes. "Dad isn't violent."

He cocks an eyebrow. "And he didn't threaten to run me over with his wheelchair."

"It was your fault. You shouldn't have lied about the Fruit Loops."

We reach the end of the alleyway and slow down. I scan the area but no one else has appeared from their house and no one has followed us.

"I don't think they phoned the police." I pull out my car keys and beep the locks open.

Kai swipes the keys from me. "You're injured. You're not driving."

I roll my eyes. "Your definition of injury is false."

I'm complaining but I enjoy how he's taking care of me. No one's taken care of me in a long time. I'm the one who's always taking care of others. The roll reversal feels good. It's nice to be taken care of.

Chapter 26

"She said she trusts me. My brain short-circuited."
~ Kai

KAI

"I'm serious, Goofy. I don't need to go to the emergency room because of a little blood."

I scowl. "It's more than a little bit of blood."

Harper shows me her elbow. "It's not even bleeding anymore."

"Fine," I give in. "But we're stopping by my house to clean it up before we go to your house. I don't want Henry seeing you bleeding."

She giggles. "Dad has seen me bleeding plenty. Who do you think taught me how to ride a bike? Or use a hammer? Or a power drill?"

"You know how to use a power drill?"

She slaps my shoulder. "Don't look so surprised. Who do you think does the repairs at *Rumrunner?*"

"Flynn." Flynn owns the local construction company. He's pretty much the handyman for everyone on the island.

She snorts. "I'm not calling Flynn every time the toilets flood at the bar. Do you know how often I have to dig a glass out of a toilet?"

"From now on, you call me."

"Kai, you don't have to solve every single problem in my life."

"Why not?"

"I don't even know how to answer that question."

I park her car in my driveway and run around the front to open her door. I try to lift her into my arms but she bats me away.

"There's nothing wrong with my legs. You're worse than my mom."

"What did your mom do?" I ask as I escort her into the house.

"She fainted at the sight of blood."

"Really?"

"The teeniest tiniest amount of blood and bam! She hit the floor."

"We would have had massive problems in my house if Mom fainted whenever one of us was bleeding."

She sighs. "I don't know how your mom survived having six sons."

"You don't want sons?"

She snorts. "Not six."

"What about two?"

"Will they take after you? Because then one is too many."

She barely admits I'm her boyfriend, but she's actually discussing her children resembling me. Progress is happening with my stubborn, grumpy lover.

I glare at her to hide my excitement. "You're mean."

"But not wrong."

We enter my bathroom and I lift her up to set her on the vanity. "Overboard, your name is Kai."

I dig through my vanity until I find my first aid kit. "If caring for you is going overboard, I plead guilty."

"You're supposed to be goofy, not charming."

"I can be both things."

I find some antiseptic swipes in the kit. "This is going to hurt a little."

"That's what he said."

I grin. "Harper Poole, did you make a dirty joke?"

"I can joke." I raise an eyebrow. "I normally don't have time to joke, but I'm perfectly capable of joking."

I wipe the wound and she winces. "Sorry. Need to clean this up before it gets infected. There are little pebbles and sand in the wound."

"You sound like an expert."

"Five brothers, remember?"

"Did you ever consider going to medical school?"

"Nah. By the time I finished college, Eli had already founded *Buccaneer's Whiskey*."

"And he chose you to be the operations manager straight out of college?"

I shrug. "I was the only brother left. Rhett is a financial wizard. Jaxon is determined to make the best whiskey ever. Miles only shows up at the distillery when the weather isn't good for surfing. And Zane comes and goes as he wills."

"Hey." She cups my chin. "Eli wouldn't have appointed you as operations manager if he didn't believe you could do the job."

I sigh. "I know. I just wish Jaxon had as much faith in me as Eli does."

Her brow wrinkles. "Jaxon doesn't have any faith in you?"

I glance away. I can't gaze into her eyes when I admit the truth. "I haven't exactly shown him I'm capable."

She pinches my chin and forces my gaze to return to hers. "Then, you change his mind by showing him you are capable."

"What makes you think I am?"

Her eyes widen. "Are you serious?"

"Forget it." I reach for a bandage but she grasps my hand to stop me.

"Kai Raider, you listen to me. Are you listening?"

I nod.

"You have proven to me you aren't merely a goofball and a jokester who's never serious. You've helped me get a handle on helping my dad. You helped Sloane, so she has more time to work. You've kicked in to work at *Rumrunner* several times so I could get some time off."

"I did those things for you."

"I know. Do whatever you need to do to show Jaxon you can not only handle being the operations manager for the distillery but you excel at it."

"What if I don't excel?"

"You learn. You ask Jaxon for advice. Sign up for some courses. You figure it out."

I blow out a breath. "You're right. I can figure it out."

"Of course, I'm right. I'm always right. Get used to it."

She smiles and both of her dimples make an appearance. I can't resist her lips. I meld my mouth to hers and she sighs. I thrust my tongue inside and groan.

I love her taste – beer and vanilla. Two of my favorite things in the world. But they can't compare to this woman. This woman believes in me despite how immature I've acted in the past.

Fuck. I love her.

She wraps her legs around me and draws me near until my hard length presses against her. She grinds herself against me and my cock weeps in response. It's been too long since I sank into heaven.

I wrench my lips from hers. "We shouldn't. You're injured."

"We should and we will." She whips her t-shirt off to reveal a teal colored satin bra.

I groan. "Your lingerie should be illegal."

"What?" She bats her eyelashes at me. "You want my lingerie to be banned?"

My thumbs massage her nipples through the satin. "I love this bra."

She plants her hands on the vanity behind her and arches into my touch. "Don't stop."

I yank the cups of the bra down to reveal her pretty pink nipples. "Not stopping," I mutter before I latch onto her nipple. I nibble and lick until it's a hard point before moving on to the other one.

She grinds against my cock. "Kai."

"Right here," I murmur against her skin.

"I need more."

"What do you need, Slugger?" All she has to do is ask, and she can have whatever she wants.

"You inside me."

I wrap my arms around her – intent on carrying her into my bedroom – but she pushes me away. "Here. Now."

"Whatever you want, Slugger. But I need to grab a condom from my bedroom."

"Not necessary."

My pulse spikes. "Not necessary?"

"I'm on the pill and I trust you."

My heart pounds in my chest. I have to force the question out. "You trust me?"

She frames my face with her hands. "I don't have sex with men I don't trust."

"I've never had sex without a condom before." My brothers would have killed me if I got a girl pregnant.

"Me neither. We can have this first together."

My cock twitches. It loves the idea of sharing a first with the woman it's obsessed with.

"If you're certain."

"I am, Goofy. I am."

While she kicks off her shoes, I unzip her jeans. She's wearing a pair of matching satin panties. "I love your panties."

I sneak my hand past the elastic, past her clit, until I reach her core. "You're already wet."

"And impatient," she grumbles. She's adorable when she's grumpy.

I thrust two fingers inside her and she moans as her inner muscles clamp down on my fingers. I nibble on her earlobe. "Shall I make you come this way?"

"Want you."

"You have me. You have all of me." More than she can possibly imagine.

"Please, Kai."

I can't resist her when she begs. I draw my fingers out and push her panties down her legs with her jeans. Once she's naked, I shove my jeans down until my cock is exposed.

She reaches for me and fists my length. I groan at how amazing it feels to have her hand wrapped around me. My lower back tingles and my balls heat. I'm close to coming from a few tugs from Harper. My stamina disappears when she's involved.

I slap her hands away. "This will be over awfully quick if you don't stop."

She smirks and her dimples make an appearance. "Are you saying you're a one-pump wonder?"

I growl. "You know damn well I'm not a one-pump wonder."

She bats her eyelashes. "I do?"

I growl. "You're going to pay for that."

"Promises. Promises."

I notch my cock at her entrance. I meet her gaze before I thrust inside until my balls slap her skin. She moans and I grit my teeth when her walls convulse around me. There's nothing between us. We're skin to skin in the most intimate way possible. I've never felt anything better.

"Damn. You feel good. Better than anything I've felt before."

"More moving. Less talking."

I slowly retreat until only the tip of my cock is inside her. I pause a second before sinking into her again. She tightens her legs around my waist and arches into every thrust.

I've never seen anything more beautiful than Harper letting go. Her hair flies behind her, her breasts bounce with every thrust, and her cheeks are dark with a blush. I will never forget this moment with her. The moment she admitted she trusts me.

We establish a rhythm. I pump into her and she meets my every thrust. It's glorious. I never want it to end. But soon enough, my lower back is tingling and her walls are tightening around me.

"I love this. I love being inside you. I love you. Period."

"Kai!" she screams as her climax hits her.

Her orgasm triggers my own. I erupt into her. No condom between us. Some day soon, I'll come into her when she isn't on the pill and we can start making babies. Because I am not letting this woman go. She's my world.

Chapter 27

"I was fine until feelings got involved. Rude." ~ *Harper*

HARPER

I stay cuddled in Kai's arms while I allow my heart rate to calm down. Oh, who am I kidding? My heart rate will not be calming down anytime soon.

Kai loves me?

No, he can't love me. He's a kid. He doesn't know what he wants.

Except Mom and Dad married when they were younger than he is now. And they were in love until the day Mom died. And then Dad had a stroke and nearly died. He nearly left me all alone.

My breath hitches and gets stuck in my throat. I can't catch my breath. My chest cramps as I try to fill my lungs.

I can't chance this. This whole relationship was supposed to be a bit of fun. I wasn't supposed to fall for Kai. Kai wasn't supposed to love me.

Escape. It's the only thing I can do.

I push away from Kai. He smiles down at me with such tenderness I want to cry. No crying, Harper. Not here. Not now.

"I need to clean up." Good excuse. It'll get me a few moments away from Kai's presence.

He kisses my nose. "I'll get some water for us."

I force myself to smile. To act as if nothing's wrong. Judging by the way his eyes narrow, Kai isn't buying it. But he doesn't say anything. He fixes his jeans and strolls out of the bathroom, shutting the door behind him.

Escape! The word pounds in my mind. I need to get out of here.

I use the facilities before donning my clothes as fast as possible. My t-shirt rips but I don't stop to check how bad it is. I can't stop now.

I fly out of the bathroom, down the hallway, and out the door. Thank the smugglers I drove today.

I'm backing out of the driveway when Kai rushes out the door. "Harper!"

I don't answer. I whip the car around and floor it.

When I'm five minutes away from Kai's house and have checked the mirrors about a dozen times to make sure he didn't follow me, I pull to the side of the road. I don't know where to go. I don't want to go home. Dad will hit me with five thousand questions. None of which I can answer.

And *Rumrunner* is out. Sloane can sniff out a secret at twenty yards.

There's only one place I can go.

I park my car near the boardwalk and make my way to the beach. *Prohibition Beach* is the place Mom loved most on Smuggler's Hideaway. Even when she was sick and could no longer walk, Dad would carry her onto the sand.

The beach is practically deserted since it's getting dark. Besides, the high season is over. It's still warm enough to swim and surf, but the crowds of tourists have returned to their homes.

I sit on the sand and hug my knees to my chest. Kai loves me? Is this puppy love or is he serious? And, if he's serious, what am I going to do?

"Is this seat taken?" Jessica asks.

I startle. I didn't hear her approach since I was lost in my thoughts.

"Hi," I greet Kai's mother.

"How are you, my dear?"

I frown at her. "Did Kai phone you?" She nods. "How did he know where I'd be?"

She shrugs. "I don't know. All I know is my son is worried about you and freaking out."

"Freaking out?"

"He's worried he's ruined his relationship with you."

I blow out a breath. "He didn't ruin anything."

She lifts her brows. "But he does have reason to worry?"

"He said he loved me," I confess instead of answering her question.

She smiles. "I could see his love for you at the barbecue."

My brow wrinkles. "You could?"

She sighs. "Kai is my baby. His older brothers and I have protected him to give him the youth they missed out on when their dad left."

I cringe. "I'm sorry your husband left you."

"I'm not going to lie and say it's not a big deal. It was a big deal. Raising six boys while working two full-time jobs was tough. I was lucky Eli and Rhett stepped up. But I'm also extremely sad my baby boys had to grow up earlier than they should of. Instead of playing football, Eli worked odd jobs while Rhett stayed at home and missed prom to help keep Jaxon, Miles, Zane, and Kai on track."

I snort. "I can't imagine Jaxon ever needed help keeping on track."

She laughs. "True. Jaxon is my little genius. It was obvious from the time he was five and returned home from kindergarten to announce he needed glasses."

"He knew he needed glasses?"

"There was an eye test and he failed. He never failed tests."

I shake my head. Sounds like Jaxon.

She clears her throat. "Anyway, I could tell by the way Kai acted that he was in love with you. My youngest has a big heart, but he's a goofball."

"I call him Goofy."

"He's not a goofball when you and your dad are around. He acts like the man of the family – taking care of your dad and you."

"My dad had a stroke after Mom died," I say instead of responding to her comments about Kai. I can't deal with how

Kai has grown up to become a man for me. It's too much to handle at the moment.

"Ah." She nods. "And now you are afraid of love."

I scowl. "I'm not afraid of love."

She meets my gaze. She doesn't have the Raider blue eyes – the color must come from their father – but her brown eyes bore into mine without blinking. I duck my chin when I can no longer meet her gaze.

"I might be afraid of losing love," I admit. "Dad after Mom died…" I blow out a breath. "He was inconsolable. And then he had the stroke."

Jessica squeezes my hand. "He didn't have a stroke because of grief."

"I know. At least, my head knows. My heart? Not so much."

"I admit I was inconsolable after Ted left. But every day it gets a bit easier. Every day, your heart hurts a little less. And then, one day, you find another man who forces his way into your heart."

"My dad never wanted another woman."

"But he didn't give up on living."

"He worked his ass off to recover from his stroke."

"And there you have it. There's no reason to be afraid of losing love."

"Ugh. You make it sound easy."

"Ha! There's nothing easy about love. But there's also nothing as rewarding as love."

I stare into the ocean. I don't love Kai. I might be falling for him. But I'm not there yet.

"Uh oh," Jessica mutters as she points to a group of men – Kai's brothers – hurrying toward us. "The cavalry has arrived."

"How bad do we need to kick his ass?" Eli asks.

"Bruises? Broken bones? Stitches? Hospital visit? What?" Rhett asks.

I hold up my hand. "Whoa. Whose ass are you kicking?"

Miles rolls his eyes. "Kai's, of course."

Zane crosses his arms over his chest. "He hurt you. He's going down."

Jaxon pushes his glasses up his nose. "You and your dad are family now. We don't let anyone hurt our family."

I get to my feet and brush the sand off of my jeans. "I'm not family."

Jessica wraps an arm around my waist. "My boy loves you. You're family."

Warmth spreads throughout my body at her declaration. I've always wanted a big family. Mom was the best, and I love my dad with all my heart, but I never had any siblings. Siblings to tease you and play with. Siblings who will rush to your side when you need them. Siblings who will support you even when you messed up.

Miles's nose wrinkles. "If Kai loves her, why did he break up with her?"

"Kai did not break up with me."

"He didn't?" Jaxon's brow wrinkles. "Why are you upset and crying on the beach if he didn't break up with you?"

I won't allow them to think Kai broke up with me – especially since they appear ready to beat him up for hurting me

– but I'm not telling them I ran away because he declared his love. Who does that? Apparently me.

"I'm not crying." Not at the moment, at least.

He leans close as if to inspect my face but Rhett pulls him back. "No."

"Harper just needed a bit of girl talk," Jessica says. "Since she doesn't have a mother anymore, I stepped in."

"Girl talk?" Zane shivers. "Count me out."

He starts to walk away. Miles chases after him. "Wait for me! The waves are calling my name."

"I should get back to Blossom. I told her I had a work emergency. She gets angry if I work on the weekends." Jaxon waves before marching off.

"Are you certain you're okay?" Eli asks.

Rhett nods. "We can hurt Kai in ways no one will notice."

"Boys," Jessica growls. "Stop threatening to harm my baby."

"It's actually kind of sweet." In a super weird and slightly scary way.

"You shouldn't encourage them. They're bad enough without the encouragement."

Eli smirks at his mom. "And you love us anyway."

Rhett wraps his arms around her and lifts her into the air. She giggles as she slaps at his shoulders to let her down.

"Do you need a ride home?" Eli asks.

"I'm good."

"Catch you later, sis." Rhett grins as he walks off with Eli and their mom.

My heart is full as I watch them make their way across the sand. They've accepted me and my grumpy dad into their family. They're not merely saying I'm family. They show it.

I blow out a breath. I guess I'd better go fix things with Kai before I lose him.

He loves me. My heart squeezes, but I'm not struggling to breathe at the thought of Kai's love for me. I'm still afraid of losing him, but Jessica helped me to put my fear into a place where I can handle it.

Chapter 28

"I said 'I love you,' Not 'Start your engines.'"
~ Kai

KAI

The front door opens and I rush from the kitchen toward it. Is Harper running away? Not on my watch. But by the time I'm on the porch, she's already in her car barreling away.

"Harper!"

Her response? She floors it and the car rockets down the street. Fuck.

I run a hand down my face. I shouldn't have love bombed her during sex. I shouldn't have love bombed her, period. She's not ready.

Now she's panicking. I'm panicking. Everyone's panicking. I do the one thing proven to help when I'm panicking.

"Kai," Mom answers on the first ring.

"I need help."

"I don't bury bodies. Call your brothers."

"Ha. Ha. Very funny. It's girl trouble."

"What did you do?" She growls, making it clear whose side she's on. Spoiler alert. It's not mine.

I can't tell her I told Harper I love her and she ran. There's not a hole small enough for me to crawl into.

"Harper's upset. She drove away."

"I'll handle this. Where is she?"

"She...." I pause when I realize I have no idea where Harper would go when she's upset. Not home. She'll avoid her dad. And not to work. I think.

"I'll message you."

"I'm on standby."

"Thanks, Mom. Love you."

"Love you, baby boy."

Great. I need to have another humiliating conversation today.

"What?" Henry answers.

"Hi, Henry. Hypothetical question. Where would Harper go if she was upset?"

"If you hurt my baby girl, I'm coming after you. Wheelchair be damned."

I cringe. I don't doubt Henry would accomplish his goal. He's as stubborn as his daughter after all.

"I didn't hurt her. I ... ah..." Damnit. I have no idea how to explain myself.

"Out with it, boy."

"I told her I love her."

"Well, shit. No wonder she ran."

"I didn't say she ran."

"But you calling me tells me she did."

I can't argue since he's right. "Where would she go?"

"Prohibition Beach. It was her mom's favorite place. She goes there to speak to her mom."

I should have known this. But every time Harper mentions her mom, she looks lost and I change the subject. That shit ends now. There will be no more holding back. That ship has sailed anyway.

"Thanks, Henry."

I hang up and message mom. And then I start pacing. Should I go to the beach with Mom? Or should I let her handle this?

I snag my keys and make my way to my SUV. Mom can handle this, but I'll be there when Harper's ready. I'll always be there. I will always wait for her. Be someone she can count on.

"Come in!" Henry yells when I knock on their door.

"Hey, Henry," I greet as I walk inside.

He nods in approval. "You showed up. I knew I liked you for a reason."

Carl strolls out of the kitchen. "Where's Harper?"

"Boy scared her and she ran off."

My cheeks warm at Henry's loud declaration.

"You waiting for her here?" Carl asks and I nod. "Excellent. I need to quit early. My kid has a dance recital."

"Go ahead." I don't hesitate to agree.

Harper can get mad at me all she wants. She needs to learn I'm here to help her. Not tell her what to do. There's a difference. Her stubbornness gets in the way of telling them apart. Lucky her. I'm here to explain.

"Dinner isn't made yet," Carl says as he waves goodbye.

"What do you want for dinner?" I ask Henry. He opens his mouth but I wag my finger. "And don't say Fruit Loops. Cereal is breakfast, not dinner."

"Fine," he grouches. "Spaghetti."

"Holler if you need anything."

He waves me away. "Shush. My show is on."

I chuckle as I get to work. I'm scooping the fried rice into a container when the door opens.

"Kai!" Harper yells.

"Keep it down," her dad grumbles. "The whole neighborhood heard you."

I can't hear Harper's reply but she barges into the kitchen moments later.

"What are you doing here?"

I motion to the counter, which is now covered in dishes. "What do you think I'm doing?"

"I think you're trying to take over my life."

I scratch my chin. "By preparing a week's worth of meals? You hate to cook."

"And she sucks at it!" Henry yells.

"Stay out of this!" Harper yells back.

"Then, keep your voice down!"

"You need to stop pushing me," she grumbles to me.

"I'm not pushing you."

She rears back. "You're not? You didn't send your mom and brothers after me?"

"Technically, I only sent my mom. She called my brothers. I didn't."

Did I know she'd call them? Yes. But I didn't actually connect the calls myself.

"Do not get technical with me, Kai Raider."

"You asked if I sent my brothers after you. I did not."

She throws her arms in the air. "This is what I mean. You push, push, push."

I prowl toward her. "And I'm not sorry. I had to be certain you were okay when you hightailed it out of my house faster than Zane runs to the bathroom after eating beans."

Her face softens. I have a feeling no one's made sure Harper is okay for a long time. Her dad loves her – it's plain to see – but she's the one caring for him, not the other way around.

Harper needs someone to care for her. I signed up for the job and I don't plan to quit. Ever.

"I love you, Slugger."

The hardness disappears from her eyes, and I dare to grasp her hand.

"I'll wait forever for you if I have to, but I will take care of you in the meantime."

She bristles. "I don't need anyone to take care of me."

"I didn't say you did."

She blows out a breath. "It's awful hard to argue with you when you keep giving me the perfect answers."

I palm her face. "I'll always give you the perfect answers. You're it for me, Harper Poole. The woman I've been waiting my whole life for."

She sniffs. "You're twenty-four."

I shrug. "Doesn't change what I said."

She swallows, and I brace for a blow. Guessing by the stubborn tilt of her jaw, whatever she wants to say is going to hurt. "What if I don't love you?"

I was wrong. It doesn't hurt. It fucking kills. I let her words burn through me. They're not true. I know it. She knows it. She's just scared.

I tuck a strand of her hair behind her ear. "You care for me, Harper. You can't deny it."

"I can if I want to."

I lean over and whisper into her ear. "Your body doesn't lie, Slugger." I kiss the skin below her ear and she moans. "I'll wait forever for you if I have to."

She arches her neck to give me more space, and I nibble her skin. She clenches the front of my t-shirt.

"What if I'm never ready?"

"Stop worrying about the future."

"One of us has to."

I sigh and retreat a step. I keep my hands on her hips – I can't stop touching her when she's near – but I give her the space she obviously needs.

"I'm not going to get cancer and leave you." I guess at why she's afraid.

She scowls. "You can't promise you won't get cancer."

"Okay." I nod since she's right. "I won't ever abandon you on purpose. I won't find another woman and start a family with her and forget all about you."

"Your dad is an asshole."

"Agreed. But there's one good thing about dear old dad."

"What?"

"I know how not to act. I will never leave you, and I will never give you a reason to leave me."

She lifts an eyebrow. "Except pushing me and taking over my life."

"Taking care of you is not the same as taking over your life and you know it. You're just being contrary because I told you I love you and it freaked you out."

She narrows her eyes at me. "I did not freak out because you told me you love me."

I bark out a laugh. "You didn't race off like you're the lead driver in the Indy 500 the second I confessed my love?"

"I put my clothes back on first," she jokes and relief fills me. The danger is over.

We'll have plenty more fights. Harper is a stubborn woman who can be as grumpy as her father. Fighting with her is unavoidable. But I will never leave her. No matter how much she fights me and my love.

She's stuck with me.

Chapter 29

"Nothing says romance like hospital chocolate and questionable life choices." ~ Harper

HARPER

Dad crosses his arms over his chest and glares at me. "I don't want to go."

"Dad."

"Don't Dad me. I'm perfectly happy staying here and watching my programs."

Kai does a dramatic sigh. "Such a shame. I was hoping I'd have someone to share a rack of ribs with. I guess I'll have to eat the whole thing myself."

I bite my tongue. I don't want Dad eating unhealthy food but as it's one of the few things to bring him joy, I can't deny him. Not when Kai's around, at least.

Dad scowls. "There aren't any ribs at *Mermaid Mini Golf*."

"But there are plenty of ribs at *Smuggler's Cove* where we're going to eat after I kick my brothers' asses at mini golf."

"Why don't we skip the mini golf?" Dad asks.

"No can do. It's family day. Family day must include a shared activity."

"Eating is a shared activity."

"Are you willing to tell my mom, eating is a shared activity?" Kai asks.

Dad grunts, which is basically his way of saying 'you're right but I'll never admit it out loud'.

I guide Dad's wheelchair to him. "Are you finished being a grump now?"

"No," he grumbles but he does allow Kai to help him into the wheelchair.

Kai wheels Dad outside, but at the top of the steps, he stops and frowns. "You really need to do something about getting a ramp."

"Dad's cast will come off soon and then we won't need a ramp."

Kai lifts his eyebrow. "The steps are easy for him to maneuver?"

I purse my lips. "Easier."

"Exactly," he mutters as he lifts Dad in his wheelchair and carries him down the steps.

I can't help but notice how his biceps bulge with the effort. Biceps I've sunk my nails into while Kai tastes my skin with his tongue – more skillful than any hero in one of my romance novels.

"Feeling warm?" Kai smirks and I realize I'm fanning my face. I drop my hand, and he chuckles.

"Whatever."

We get Dad situated in Kai's SUV and begin driving out of town toward *Mermaid Mini Golf*. Kai's phone rings and he answers.

"The island's about to get one smuggler louder!" Miles shouts.

"On our way." Kai ends the call and speeds up.

"What's going on?"

"Paisley's in labor."

"Good. We can go straight to the restaurant," Dad says.

Kai chuckles. "Sorry, Henry. Hospital first."

The hospital isn't far. It's halfway between Smuggler's Rest and Rogue's Landing, which – on an island the size of Smuggler's Hideaway – is equal to a five-minute drive.

As we're crossing the parking lot, Miles and Zane arrive.

Zane rubs his hands together. "I'm going to win."

I frown at him. "Win?"

"The bet. Duh."

I roll my eyes. "I should have known."

The Raider brothers love their betting. They had a whole bet going on when Kai and I would get together. And, no, I don't know who won. And I don't want to.

"Mr. P!" Miles shouts in greeting to my dad before commandeering his wheelchair from Kai. "How fast does this thing go?"

I chase after them as Miles runs with Dad in the wheelchair. "Be careful!"

We reach the entrance to the hospital and they're forced to slow down. I elbow Miles until he releases the wheelchair.

"You're no fun," he mumbles.

"That's what she said."

His eyes widen before he barks out a laugh. "Trust me." He drapes an arm over my shoulders. "She has never said I'm not fun."

"Really?" I raise my eyebrows. "Not even Hazel?"

He scowls before storming through the doors ahead of us.

Kai shakes his head. "You weren't kidding when you said you know all the gossip in Smuggler's Hideaway."

I roll my eyes. "It's not a big secret how Miles broke Hazel's heart and now she hates him with the intensity of a mermaid scorned."

Zane smiles as he passes me. "You're a fun addition to the family."

Warmth spreads throughout me at his proclamation, and I beam at him. "Thanks."

"Come on!" Miles motions at us from where he's standing in front of the elevators, waiting for us.

The waiting room is full when we reach it. Rhett and Dakota and Jaxon and Blossom are already here.

"I was promised ribs," Dad grumps when I park his wheelchair in the waiting room.

"How about a crappy coffee and a half-melted candy bar?"

It was our dinner of choice when Mom was in the hospital for one of her treatments. Mom didn't allow me coffee or chocolate, so it was our little secret.

His smile is wonky. "Thanks, Harp."

Kai grasps my hand. "I'll go with you."

"Behave, Dad," I order.

We barely make it out of the waiting room before a door flies open and Stuart appears.

"I'm trying to help!" he shouts back into the room.

"You're not helping!" Jessica yells back at him.

"Two guesses which room Paisley's in," Kai whispers to me.

"No one's helping!" Paisley screams.

"Ding. Ding. Ding. We have a winner."

I elbow him. "Knock it off."

Stuart shakes his head at me. "Be warned. The people in this family are crazy."

I've lived my entire life on Smuggler's Hideaway. Some would claim all of the islanders are crazy. I've seen a lot of crazy. I'm comfortable with crazy.

"Eli Raider, you are not a doctor. Put down my chart and stop ordering your mother around," Paisley yells from within the room.

Kai tugs on my hand. "Let's go before we have to phone the police over a domestic disturbance."

"Wow. You really don't enjoy living, do you?" I ask but allow him to lead me away.

We arrive at a bank of vending machines.

"What do you want?"

"Nothing from here." I point upward. "The best vending machines are on the fifth floor."

"And here I thought I knew everything there was to know about this hospital."

"Dad and I spent a lot of time here when Mom was getting her treatments."

He squeezes my hand as we climb the stairs to the fifth floor.

"I wish I could have met her."

"Mom would have loved you. She wouldn't have known what to do with you, but she would have loved you."

He pins me to the wall next to the door to the fifth floor. "As long as you know what to do with me."

His gaze dips to my mouth and I push up on my toes to press my lips to his. It's a brief kiss. I won't be making out in a stairwell at the hospital, no matter how much I enjoy those hospital television shows where everyone is sleeping with everyone.

When we return to the maternity ward, I nearly get run over by Zane in a wheelchair. Miles isn't far behind him.

"Be careful," Kai growls at them.

"What are you doing in a wheelchair?" I ask.

"Duh. It's the wheelchair Olympics." Zane grins. "And I'm winning."

"Maybe I let you win," Miles grumbles but everyone ignores him.

I hand Kai the coffees and chocolate bars we purchased. "What events are there?"

"We're currently racing. Whoever can make it down the hallway in a wheelchair the fastest wins."

I motion for him to get up. "I'm in. I assume the only rule is there are no rules."

I settle in the wheelchair while Kai settles in Miles's wheelchair.

"Ready. Set. Go!" Miles shouts.

I set off down the corridor using my hands and feet to increase my pace.

"You're cheating," Kai says. "No using your feet."

I ram my wheelchair into his. "I thought there were no rules."

His eyes narrow. "I'm going to get you."

"You can try!" I sing as I rocket down the corridor. He tries to catch up to me, but I weave back and forth to stop him from passing me.

"Harper Poole, you are devious."

I reach the end of the hallway and throw my hands in the air. "I'm the winner is what I am."

Kai jumps from his chair and hauls me out of mine into his arms. "I love watching you let loose," he whispers before his lips meld to mine. I sigh and he thrusts his tongue into my mouth. His whiskey and worn flannel scent surrounds me and I melt into him.

I could do this all day. And all night, for that matter. I love the taste of his lips. I love how his scent smells of home. I love how safe I feel in his arms. I love how he makes me feel not alone.

I love…

I need to stop with the love thing. I don't love Kai. It's too soon. He's too young.

"Hey, lovebirds!" Rhett hollers and Kai grunts before releasing me.

"What?"

"The baby's here."

Kai's eyes light up. "The baby's here."

He tags my hand and drags me to Paisley's hospital room. The room is crowded with the entire Raider family. Even my dad is in here.

Paisley is laying in the bed holding a tiny human being while Eli leans over her. He smiles at the baby and the love practically pours out of him.

Eli lifts the baby from her. "Family, meet Stephanie Raider."

Jessica bursts into tears. "Stephanie was my mother's name." Stuart wraps an arm around her and she buries her face into his shoulder.

The baby is handed from uncle to uncle until she reaches Kai. Kai smiles down at her. "Hi, little Raider. Welcome to the world. You don't know me yet, but I'm your Uncle Kai. I'm going to be your favorite uncle."

He kisses her nose and I sigh. I can't wait for him to kiss the nose of our children. He'll be the best dad ever.

Welp. I guess it's official. I am no longer falling for Kai. I love him. My heart hammers in my chest as fear creeps in. I hope I'm not making a mistake, but I have no choice in the matter. My heart latched onto Kai before my mind could stop it.

"Does this mean it's time for ribs now?" Dad asks and the room bursts into laughter.

Chapter 30

"Look, I said I'd be quiet. I never said she would." ~ Kai

KAI

"I'm tired. I'm going to bed," Henry announces when a commercial break comes on.

It's only nine but I can't blame him. It's been a long day. First, the hospital and then dinner at *Smuggler's Cove* to celebrate our new niece. Dinner with the Raider brothers is never quiet or short.

Harper yawns as she pushes to her feet. "Let's go."

"Kai can help me."

"Dad."

"I said Kai can help me."

I stand. "I got this, Slugger."

I kiss Harper before making my way to Henry. I wheel him down the hallway to his bedroom, where I help him get changed into pajamas and ready for bed.

"If you need anything, shout."

"All I ask is for you to be quiet."

I nearly choke on air at his words. For a grumpy man, those words are a ringing approval, complete with five stars and a thumbs-up.

I wink at him. "Got ya."

I nearly bump into Harper at the end of the hallway, where she's pacing and wringing her hands. I capture her hand and kiss her palm.

"He's fine, Slugger."

"I know. It's just hard. I've always been the one to care for him."

I brush the hair off of her forehead. "It's hard to let go, but you couldn't keep going the way you were." Her jaw tightens but I continue before she has a chance to let her grump loose. "You were killing yourself. Your dad wants you to have a life, too."

Her shoulders slump with defeat. "I know."

I wrap an arm around her shoulders and guide her toward her bedroom. She plants her feet when we reach the door. "What are you doing?"

"Getting ready for bed."

"You can't sleep here."

"As a matter of fact, I can."

"No, Kai. This isn't a joke. I don't invite men to sleep over when my dad is here."

"Men?" I growl. "I'm not some random stranger. I'm the man who loves you. Who plans to spend his life with you."

She squirms. "But my dad."

"Told us to be quiet."

She gasps. "What?"

I push her into her room and shut the door behind us. "Your dad said we should be quiet."

She groans. "You spoke to my dad about having sex with me in the house?"

I chuckle, and she glares at me. I hold up my hands. "Sorry. Henry brought it up."

She collapses on the bed and buries her face in her hands. "How am I ever going to look Dad in the eye again?"

I pry her hands away from her face. "I hate to break it to you, Slugger. But Henry knows you have sex."

"Knowing and seeing are two different beasts."

I kneel between her legs. "He's going to figure out we're having sex when I knock you up."

She narrows her eyes at me. "Knock me up?"

I shrug. "It'll happen eventually."

"What if I don't want children?"

"Slugger. Slugger. Slugger." I shake my head. "Don't lie to me. I know you too well."

"What do you know?"

"I know you damn near melted when you held little Stephanie for the first time today. I know you've missed having a family. I know you want a big family."

"I am not having six boys."

I chuckle. "I wouldn't want you to but would two be so bad?"

"If they're like you and your brothers, yes."

"Having the next generation of Raider boys would be a blast."

She crosses her arms over her chest. "You're going to change their diapers, feed them in the middle of the night, discipline them when they get in trouble at school?"

"Depends on the trouble."

"I'm serious, Goofy."

"I'm serious, too. I plan to be a hands-on dad. I want to experience every moment possible with our kids." My jaw tightens. "I am not going to be my dad."

"You are nothing like your dad. You might be a total goofball, but you look after the people you care for."

Her words hit me straight in the chest. They mean the world to me.

I don't remember much about my dad. Not only because he left when I was ten. But also because he wasn't around before then. He certainly didn't help Mom raise us boys. The last thing I want to be is him.

"Thanks, Slugger."

"I..." She trails off to yawn.

I help her to her feet. "Come on. Time for bed. You're exhausted."

"You're not going to leave, are you?"

I pinch her chin. "If you can look me in the eyes and tell me you want me to leave, I'll leave."

She meets my gaze. Her light blue eyes sparkle but I'm uncertain whether the sparkle is anger or mirth.

"Fine. You can stay. But no sexy times."

I smirk. "You can't resist me."

She snorts. "I think it's you who can't resist me."

She walks toward the attached bathroom. "I need to get ready for bed." She whips off her shirt, revealing a red lace bra.

My cock twitches and I groan. "Tease."

"You're the one who wants to stay," she sings before shutting the door.

I rub a hand down my face as I try to get my cock under control. She said no sex, I remind it. She also threw her shirt at me and showed off her sexy bra, it reminds me. Good point.

I remove my shirt and jeans and crawl into bed. I find the remote control and switch on the television as I wait for Harper. Women always need loads of time to get ready for bed. Skincare regimes and I don't know what.

I haven't clicked through the first round of channels before Harper strolls out of the bathroom. My jaw drops to the floor and my cock springs into action when I get a look at what she's wearing – a black satin nightgown. It's floor length but when she moves the slit in the side showcases her leg from her ankle to her thigh.

"I thought you didn't want to have sex," I manage to croak out.

"Who said I want to have sex?"

I groan. "You can't be serious. You can't stroll into the bedroom wearing the sexiest nightgown in existence and expect me not to jump you."

She sways from side to side, showing off that fucking tempting slit and I swear. "You're not wearing any underwear."

Her nose wrinkles. "I don't wear bras to bed. Too uncomfortable."

"You're not wearing panties."

My cock is now fully erect and peaking from the top of my boxer shorts. It doesn't give a smuggler's hoot about my promise to keep my hands to myself. It wants to bury itself deep in her pussy and it wants it now. I don't disagree.

"Get your sexy ass over here."

She bats her eyelashes. "Or what?"

"Or I won't make sure you're quiet when you come."

She hesitates and I realize I messed up by reminding her how her dad is in the bedroom two doors down.

I roll out of bed and prowl toward her. Her gaze dips to my cock and she licks her lips. It weeps in response.

"Slugger," I growl as I draw my hands up the sides of the nightgown. She shivers in response. "You have three choices here."

"What are they?" she asks when I pause.

"I can gag you to keep you quiet when you scream for me."

"Or?"

"You can promise to be quiet when I sink into your pussy and claim what's mine."

"O-o-or?"

"Or I can walk out the door and come back in the morning."

She squeezes my dick through my boxers. "You'd leave now?"

I allow myself to enjoy the feel of her hand on me for a second before I bat her hand away. "I would. If you're uncomfortable with the situation, I'll leave. I don't ever want you to feel uncomfortable."

She blows out a breath. "I'm not uncomfortable."

I cock a brow.

"Okay, fine. I am uncomfortable, but I shouldn't be. I'm thirty-two. I'm not a virgin. I should be able to have sex in the house I live in."

I palm her face. "Am I gagging you, or can you be quiet?"

"I can be quiet."

"Challenge accepted," I mutter before molding my lips to hers. She sighs and I thrust my tongue inside. Her beer and vanilla flavor hits me and I groan before wrapping an arm around her. I drag her close until I can feel the satin of her nightgown against my naked chest.

I wrench my lips from hers before nibbling and biting my way across her jaw to her ear. "I'm going to fuck you while you're wearing this nightgown."

"Have at it, Goofy."

I grasp the hem of the nightgown and bunch the fabric up to reveal her naked legs. My mouth waters when I reach her hips. No panties. Harper is naked and on display for me.

Fuck yeah.

I lift her up and set her on the chest of drawers. Several items fall over but I ignore them. I'll replace whatever breaks but I'm not pausing in my quest to show Harper she's mine.

"Spread."

Satisfaction fills me when she doesn't hesitate to widen her legs.

"I want to taste you, but you're loud when I'm eating you out."

Her chest heaves, and her breasts bounce. "I can be quiet."

I nip her bottom lip. "Liar."

She opens her mouth to protest but I sink a finger into her and she moans instead. Her head falls back, and her chest arches toward me.

"Ride my finger."

She clamps onto my shoulders and starts riding me. Meanwhile, I can't resist those pretty breasts bouncing and teasing me.

I nibble on her nipple through the satin material and she increases her pace. I add a finger and her inner walls tighten around me. As much as I'd love to get her off twice tonight, there's no way I can keep her quiet through two orgasms. One is challenging enough.

I withdraw my fingers and she mewls. "Why are you stopping?"

I lick my fingers before dropping my boxers. "Because my cock is jealous of my fingers."

Her mouth drops open. "Oh."

I line my cock up with her opening. "No condom." We already had this discussion but I will never abuse Harper's trust. "You okay with me going bare inside you?"

She bobs her head. "Yep."

I inch inside and she moans. I love how vocal she is for me, but I don't want her to be embarrassed tomorrow with her dad.

I meld my mouth to hers as I sink my cock into her until I bottom out.

"Love you, Harper," I whisper against her lips. "Love the little sounds you make. The way your fingers dig into my biceps. And I fucking love making you come."

And then I proceed to do exactly that.

Chapter 31

"Nothing says 'Good Morning' like a well-timed guilt trip." ~ Harper

HARPER

I snuggle into Kai and his arm tightens around my waist.

He kisses my hair. "Good morning, Slugger. How did you sleep?"

I open my mouth to tell him okay but then I realize I'd be lying. I slept better than okay.

"Pretty good," I hedge. "I usually don't sleep well because of Dad's snoring."

The earplugs he bought me are great, but they're almost too great. I'm afraid Dad will call out to me and I won't hear him when I wear them.

"I'll have to fuck you to sleep more often."

I roll over to glare at him. "Awful presumptuous of you."

"I love you. I'm not sleeping apart from you."

My heart batters in my chest. This man loves me. And I love him. When he cradled baby Stephanie in his arms with such tenderness, the ice around my heart cracked wide open and love for him poured in.

I open my mouth to confess my feelings but the words get stuck in my throat. I've never told anyone I've loved them before other than my parents.

He kisses my forehead. "It's okay, Harper. I get it."

"What precisely do you get?"

"How your love for me has you tongue tied."

I bristle. "I never said I love you."

He tucks a strand of hair behind my ear. "You let me have sex with you in your bedroom two doors down from your dad. It's pretty obvious. Especially since you seduced me."

"I did not seduce you."

I didn't. It was more tempting than seducing. Besides, I love pretty nightgowns and lingerie. I have to wear them sometimes.

He chuckles. "Okay. You didn't seduce me. But you do love me."

"I…" I trail off with a sigh. "Fine. I love you. I don't know why. You're the most annoying person I've ever known. You don't understand the word no. You push and push until you get what you want. You think being a goofball is an honor."

He wraps an arm around my waist and hauls me close. "And yet, you love me."

I gaze into his stunning blue eyes and all I see is happiness. My heart clenches in my chest. This is what I've always wanted. Since the moment I understood how much my parents loved each other, I've yearned for what they had.

I didn't expect to find love with a goofball who's eight years my junior but here we are.

"Yea."

"I love you, Slugger." He melds his lips to mine. He smells of whiskey and worn flannel and home. Kai is my home.

I dig my fingers into his shoulders as he plunges his tongue into my mouth and deepens the kiss. My tongue duels with his and he growls as he grinds his hard length into my stomach. I throw my leg over his hips and—

"Harper! Where did you hide my Fruit Loops this time?" Dad shouts.

I wrench my lips from Kai's and bury my face in his chest. "I love my dad. I swear I do. But I don't like him very much right now."

He chuckles as he kisses my hair. "I'll get him settled with his cereal while you get dressed."

"You don't have to. He isn't your responsibility."

Sparks fly from his ocean blue eyes. "Henry is your dad. You're the woman I love. Hence, he's partly my responsibility."

"Hence? When did you learn the word hence?" I tease since I don't know how to deal with all these big feelings I'm feeling.

He tickles my ribs. "You think you can tease me?"

I bat at his hands. "Stop. Stop. I'll wet myself."

He shackles my wrists. "I'll stop. But only because I need to help Henry or he'll blow the whole house down with his shouting."

I groan. "You aren't wrong."

He kisses my nose before releasing me to jump out of bed. I lay back to watch him walk around the room. He leans over to pick up his jeans and I nearly groan at how spectacular his ass looks as the muscles bunch.

"Are you ogling me?"

"Someone's enjoying showing off his vocabulary this morning."

He pulls up his jeans. "Someone's good at avoiding questions this morning."

"Harper!" Dad shouts and gives me the perfect opportunity to continue avoiding his questions.

"You better go help Dad. I'm going to grab a quick shower."

"There's no rush. I've got this."

I wait until he shuts the door behind him to collapse back in the bed. I told Kai I loved him and nothing bad happened. No earthquake hit. No hurricane appeared. Nada bad shit.

In fact, good stuff was about to happen until my dad interrupted. I throw an arm over my face as I feel my cheeks warm with a blush. I can't believe I had sex in my childhood bedroom with Dad two doors down.

I debate hiding in the bedroom until it's time to go to work, but it isn't fair to force Kai to care for Dad. Besides, I'm an adult. I'm allowed to have sex. And it wasn't sex with some random man. Kai is the man I love.

Enough with these big feelings this morning. I don't know if my heart can handle more.

When I stroll into the kitchen ten minutes later, Dad is sitting at the table eating his Fruit Loops while Kai reads on his phone across from him. Kai notices me and starts to stand. "I made coffee."

I motion for him to stay seated. "I've got it."

"Good morning, Dad." I squeeze his shoulder as I pass him. "How did you sleep?"

He grunts, which could mean anything from 'I slept like crap' to 'I slept like a baby after drinking a drop of Smuggler's Hideaway moonshine'.

"I slept well. Thanks for asking," I say as I pour myself a cup of coffee.

"I bet you did."

I brace. Here we go. The guilt trip is incoming.

"I slept pretty well myself," Kai says. If he's trying to derail Dad, reminding him we slept together in my childhood bedroom is not the way to go about it.

"Are you moving in?"

I choke on my coffee at Dad's question. I cough and liquid flies from my mouth all over the counter. Kai rushes to me and slaps my back.

"I'm fine." More shocked than a smuggler who catches his first glimpse of a mermaid, but fine nonetheless.

"Well," Dad pushes once we're seated at the table. "Are you moving in or what?"

"Dad."

"We haven't discussed it," Kai says.

Dad nods. "Good. You should get married first anyway."

"Married?" I set my cup of coffee on the table. At this rate, I'm going to have a coffee bath before I can drink it.

"You know what marriage is. And I expect Kai to ask for your hand in marriage."

"I will, Henry."

I glare at Kai.

"What? If he wants me to ask for your hand in marriage, I will."

"We went from you moving in to us getting married faster than a mermaid can swim." And mermaids can swim fast. There's a reason they're not allowed to compete in the Olympics after all.

He shrugs. "We love each other. Moving in, marriage, babies. It's all going to happen."

I gasp. "You did not say we love each other in front of my dad."

Dad grunts. "If you don't love him, he shouldn't be spending the night."

I bury my face in my hands. Can I start this morning over? No, not this morning. Last night. I should have kicked Kai out when I had the chance.

But no. He has to be all sexy and hard to resist. Stupid hormones.

Kai pulls my hands away from my face. "There's nothing to be ashamed of."

"I'm not ashamed. I'm embarrassed. Two different emotions. You should know since you were beyond eager to show off your expanded vocabulary this morning."

"Is vocabulary code for something?" Dad asks and Kai bursts into laughter. I elbow him.

"What? It was funny."

"Are you two ganging up on me now?"

"You better get used to it if I'm moving in here."

"No one asked you to move in."

He points at Dad. "He kind of did."

"What about your house?"

He shrugs. "I'll sell it. Or maybe rent it out. The rental market on the island is good considering the amount of tourists who visit Smuggler's Hideaway. I'll contact my realtor. Jade lives next door, doesn't she?"

"Slow your smugglers. We haven't agreed on anything."

He shrugs. "No worries. I can be patient."

I groan. "You're doing it again."

He widens his eyes in an attempt to appear innocent. As if. Kai was born a menace. "Doing what?"

"Being pushy."

"I can't help it if I know what I want and I go all out to get it."

Warmth travels through my body at his words. Me. I'm what he wants. And he didn't stop until he got me. I only hope he won't get bored since the chase is over now and he has me.

Chapter 32

"I asked for backup, not boy band chaos." ~ *Kai*

KAI

I open the door and smile at my brothers.

Zane rubs his hands together. "What's up? What are you planning?"

"It's about time we upped the stakes in the prank war," Miles adds.

I step onto Harper's porch and shut the door behind me. "I said I needed help with Harper's dad."

"Which is code for I have the best prank idea in the world, right?" Miles wiggles his eyebrows.

"Um, no."

"Is it code for you want to have a threesome?" Zane's nose wrinkles. "I'm not down with that. Correction. I'm down to have a threesome but not with my brother."

"Ew. Me neither." Miles starts to walk away but I shackle his wrist to stop him.

"No one is having a threesome."

"I don't know," Zane says. "Since you brought the idea up, I'm considering it."

"I didn't bring it up!"

"Keep it down out there!" Henry yells.

I motion toward the house. "This is why you're here. I'm taking Harper out on a date but his caretaker, Carl, couldn't make it tonight."

Miles frowns. "I'm not a babysitter."

"So much for brothers who are always willing to help you out," I mutter. "I can't ask Eli since Stephanie is still a baby. Rhett and Dakota have enough going on with Pearl and Mira. I guess I'll ask Jaxon and Blossom."

"Jaxon's still at work."

I scowl at Zane. "Blossom then."

I dig my phone out but pause when Miles and Zane burst into laughter. "What's funny?"

Zane points at me. "Your face."

"He looks constipated," Miles says.

"You're fucking with me?"

Miles claps my shoulder. "Duh."

I should have known. Zane and Miles are shit stirrers to their cores. "Come in." I open the door and usher them inside.

"Hey, Mr. P." Miles waves at Henry.

Harper enters the living room and I forget how to breathe. She's wearing a tight, red dress that hugs all her curves. Curves I've touched and tasted. Curves, I can't wait to get my hands on again.

Zane chuckles next to me. "Dude, breathe."

I stalk toward Harper. "You're beautiful, Slugger."

She blushes and I can't resist trailing a finger from her cheek down her neck to the top of her chest. Goosebumps follow in my wake. I kiss her cheek before whispering, "I can't wait to fuck you with this dress on."

"It's a good thing I didn't wear panties, then."

My cock springs to life. It goes from half hard to fully erect with such speed, I'm dizzy from the loss of blood flow to my brain.

"You're a tease." The words come out strangled.

"You told me – and I quote here – put on something sexy enough to tease a smuggler into giving up his loot." She wiggles her shoulders, and I groan when I realize she's not wearing a bra either.

"Mission accomplished." I readjust my cock in my pants and she smirks. "Trouble."

I wrap an arm around her and lead her toward the door. She stumbles to a halt when she notices Zane and Miles standing in the living room next to her dad.

"What are they doing here?"

"They're going to watch your dad while we go out."

Her mouth gapes open. "Zane and Miles – your brothers who think advisory warnings are for losers – are going to watch Dad?"

"Advisory warnings are totally for losers," Zane says.

I glare at him. "You're not helping things."

"What?" He shrugs. "It's true."

Harper fists her hands on her hips. "Okay. Here are the rules for this evening. One. No wheelchair races in the house. Or outside of the house, either. Two. No sword fights with Dad's canes. Three. Make sure Dad gets a healthy dinner. And, finally, no feeding Dad Fruit Loops no matter how much he bitches and whines."

"I don't bitch or whine," Henry claims. I bite my tongue before I laugh since he's totally lying.

Zane whips out a Boy Scout salute. "We promise to be good."

Harper snorts. "You weren't ever a Boy Scout."

"I could have been, but I got blackballed."

Miles laughs. "Blackballed? Is that what we're calling getting kicked out for trying to start a badge for best male stripper?"

Harper groans. "Maybe we should stay home."

I usher her toward the door. "No way. I made reservations."

I rush her to my SUV and drive away before she has the chance to protest further.

"Where are we going anyway?" she asks once we're driving.

"We're driving away from Smuggler's Rest."

"*Hideaway Haven Resort*."

She gasps. "We can't go there."

Hideaway Haven is an exclusive resort built by Hudson Clark, a former NFL player who grew up on the island. It has a restaurant, various pools, a private beach, as well as a hotel and secluded cabins.

"Why not? Is there a disturbance in the universe preventing us from driving there?"

She slaps my shoulder. "No. It's too expensive."

"It's my treat."

"Your paying doesn't make it cost any less."

"I want to celebrate."

"Celebrate what?"

I place my hand on her thigh and squeeze. "How much you love me. How much I love you."

"I think we celebrated when you ripped my panties off me."

My cock twitches at the reminder of the other day. When Henry was away at physical therapy, we got some time to play.

No panties to rip off of her today. How I'd love to pull over to the side of the road and explore. But Harper deserves a special night out. She works incredibly hard and doesn't get a chance to do fun things often enough.

Good thing I'm here to ensure fun things are on the agenda more often.

"I'll replace your panties," I growl.

"You don't need to replace my panties. You don't need to spend money on expensive dinners for me."

I guess I'll be pulling over after all.

Once I'm parked at the side of the road, I pinch her chin and force her to meet my gaze. "I don't need to do jack shit. I want to spend money on you. I want to spoil you."

"Spending large amounts of money makes me uncomfortable."

This is a big admission for Harper. It warms me how much she's coming to trust me.

"I understand. And I promise not to burn money unnecessarily. We won't go out for fancy dinners every week. But when we have a reason to celebrate, you can bet your ass I'll be treating you to a fancy dinner at a fancy restaurant."

"I'm not with you for your money."

My head rears back. "I never said you were. Did someone say you are? Who are they? I need their contact details."

"No one said anything…" She trails off with a sigh. "I want you to know I'm with you because of you."

"I know you are." I waggle my eyebrows. "You couldn't resist my charm."

She groans. "Drive to the restaurant before I change my mind and insist we get burgers at *Salty Siren*."

"Your dad would kill us for getting burgers without him." I put the car in gear.

"Stop!" She flings her door open and jumps out. I chase after her.

I slow down when I realize the reason for her fear. Sammy.

The seal barks at me and I wave in return. "Hey, Sammy. You scared my woman."

He barks again. I swear, if seals could talk, he'd claim there's no way Harper could be my woman.

"I know," Harper says. "I can hardly believe we're together either."

I snatch her wrist and pull her closer to me and further away from Sammy. He's a friendly seal but he's still a wild animal. She shouldn't get too close.

Sammy barks and Harper wags a finger at him. "No backtalk. Now, get off of the road before we call the dog catchers."

The seal growls but he does scoot off of the road, so he won't get run over. We wave goodbye to him before getting back into my vehicle and recommencing our journey to the resort.

I park in front of the restaurant but Harper makes no move to get out of the SUV. She stares at the building with her mouth gaping open.

"I thought we were going to *Smuggler's Cove* to eat. I don't think I'm appropriately dressed."

"Are you kidding?" She narrows her eyes on me and I hold up my hands. "Sorry. I meant to say. You look gorgeous and I'm proud to walk into this restaurant with you on my arm."

She smooths down the skirt of her dress. "If you're certain."

"I'm more than certain. Every man in there is going to be envious of me tonight." I grasp her hand and kiss her knuckles. "But if you're uncomfortable, we'll leave."

"And miss our celebration?"

My blood heats at the taunt in her voice. "There's more than one way to celebrate."

Her breath hitches. "I have the ripped panties to prove it."

"What'll it be, Harper?"

She clears her throat. "I've always wanted to eat here."

"Your wish is my command."

I jump out, hurry around to open her door, and offer her my hand. The slit in her dress parts, showing off her curvy legs as she stands. I groan.

My cock is hard and heavy. It's going to be a long dinner if it doesn't calm down. She smiles at me, her dimples make an appearance, her blue eyes light up, and I no longer give a fuck how uncomfortable I'm going to be. I want all of her smiles directed at me. I want to give her things she hasn't had before.

I want to give her the world.

And I will.

One day at a time.

Chapter 33

"Sure, let's add a meltdown to my to-do list." ~
Harper

HARPER

"You got everything you need, Dad?"

He scowls at me. "Go. Leave me alone."

I wring my hands. I can't leave Dad alone. He can barely pick up a glass of water by himself, let alone use the toilet.

Carl is sick today and Kai volunteered to help out. But he's not here yet. I check my watch. He's already thirty minutes late. I try calling him again.

This is Kai. You know what to do.

I start to disconnect the call but decide I should probably leave a message instead.

"Where are you, Kai?" I hiss into the phone. "You were supposed to be here thirty minutes ago. I'm late for work. I can't leave Dad alone."

I stab the button to disconnect the call but it doesn't make me feel any better.

I pace in front of the window for a few minutes before picking up my phone again.

"Hey, boss lady," Sloane answers on the first ring.

"I'm running late."

"I kind of figured you were late when you didn't show up thirty minutes ago for the beer delivery."

Shoot a smuggler. I forgot all about the beer delivery.

"Did you check the delivery? Ensure we received everything we ordered?"

"Yes and yes. All good."

"I don't know when I'll be in."

"Everything okay?"

No, everything is most definitely not okay.

"Yep," I lie. "Everything's fine. I'll work on the payroll from here and be in later."

"We've got you covered, boss lady."

I wish I could believe her – despite her recent improvements, Sloane isn't the most reliable of workers – but I'm out of options.

I hang up and settle at the kitchen table with my laptop. Kai told me I should keep my laptop at the bar. That I should create a boundary between work and home.

Ha! Kai also told me he'd be here at 2 p.m. sharp this afternoon to care for my dad.

"What the hell are you doing?" Dad asks.

"Payroll."

"Why?"

Because I enjoy watching money disappear from the *Rumrunner*'s bank accounts? I swallow those words. It's not my employees' fault that I paid too much for the bar and am now struggling.

The accounts are currently healthy after the summer season, but this money needs to last throughout the winter when there are fewer tourists visiting Smuggler's Hideaway.

"Go to the bar, Harper," Dad orders in his most grumpy tone.

"I'm not leaving you alone."

"Kai will be here soon."

He will? He's already nearly an hour late. I decide to message him.

Where are you?
You're nearly an hour late.
I can't leave Dad alone.

All of my messages go unanswered.

I set my phone down and inhale a deep breath. It's okay. I'm okay. The bar isn't going to burn down because I'm an hour late. I was planning to do payroll in my office during the downtime anyway.

Payroll. Right.

I get back to work. But I can't concentrate. I check the time at least once every five minutes. Oh, who am I kidding? I'm checking it every thirty seconds and getting madder by the minute.

Seventeen minutes and thirty-three seconds later – yes, I timed it – the door opens and Kai strolls into the house.

I jump to my feet. "Where have you been?"

"I...ah..." He drags his hand through his hair. "I overslept."

"Overslept? Overslept? It's past three in the afternoon. What did you do last night?"

Normally, Kai visits me at the bar when I'm working but he didn't last night. He was probably out with his brothers, causing chaos. Silly me. I thought he'd grown up. I'm such an idiot. Such a fool.

"I never should have trusted you. I knew better. You're way too young. You don't take anything serious. You think life is a great big joke."

"Be fair, Slugger."

He starts toward me but I hold up a hand to stop him.

"Fair? What does fair even mean? Is it fair, my mom died when I was a teenager? Is it fair, Dad had a stroke a year later? Is it fair, I have to take care of every damn thing?"

"Hey!" Dad shouts. "Leave me out of this."

My cheeks heat up with embarrassment. I'm having it out with my boyfriend in front of my dad. Can things get more humiliating?

"I never should have trusted you. You will never grow up."

Kai growls. "I didn't break your trust."

I throw my arms in the air. "Didn't break my trust? I trusted you to show up here to watch my dad so I can go to work."

"I'm here now. Go on to work. Henry and I will be fine."

I'm shaking my head before he finishes. "No way. I can't trust you with Dad."

His shoulders fall and hurt clouds his blue eyes. A pang of guilt hits me but I ignore it. I'm not the cause of his pain. He brought this on himself when he didn't show up when he promised he would.

"Come on, Slugger. So, I'm a bit late. It's not the end of the world."

"Maybe not. But it is the end of us."

"Hold on. You're breaking up with me because I made one mistake?"

"One mistake?" I wince at how I'm screeching but I can't seem to stop myself. "One. You didn't show up on time. Two. You didn't answer my phone calls. Three. You didn't respond to my messages. Do you want me to go on?"

"My phone battery died. I didn't receive your calls or messages."

"Your phone battery died? Another stupid excuse." I point to the door. "Just get out. I can't look at you right now."

"You're kicking me out? What about your dad?"

"Now, you care? You didn't care for the past two hours while I worried you were lying dead in a ditch. But you were totally fine sleeping off your hangover with a dead phone."

"I didn't—"

"No. I'm done with your excuses. Please leave."

"But we'll discuss this later?"

"No, Kai. We won't. Whatever this is." I motion between the two of us. "Is over. I have no time for little boys who can't fulfill their promises."

"I am not a little boy."

"I don't have time to argue with you. I need to get Dad dressed to take with me to the bar since I don't have anyone to watch him."

"Can I drink beer and eat peanuts?" Dad asks.

"As if I could stop you." Even if I could, my employees would ply him full of liquor and bar food he shouldn't be eating.

Kai makes his way to the door but stops with his hand on the handle. "This isn't over."

"Yes, it is."

He flinches but I ignore his pain. He caused this. There's no reason for me to feel guilty. This is his fault. I never should have given in to him. Never got snared by those ocean blue eyes. Never fell for those sweet lines of his.

Lesson learned.

"Bye, Henry," Kai says and Dad waves to him as he leaves.

Once the door is closed behind him, I fly into action. I get Dad changed in record time and am wheeling him out of the house within fifteen minutes.

I screech to a halt at the top of the steps. Because there are no steps. Where the steps were, there is now a ramp with a sturdy handrail.

"Where the hell did this come from?" Dad asks.

Screw the smuggler. Since it's highly unlikely mermaids came ashore last night and performed a miracle, there's only one place the ramp could come from. Kai's been bugging me about getting a ramp since the first time he carried Dad up the stairs.

But how did he get this built and placed without me noticing? There wasn't a ramp here when I arrived home last night at three in the morning.

"I think Kai built it," I admit as I wheel Dad down the ramp to my car.

"You should have let him explain himself."

"I was too mad to hear him out."

"Told you your temper would get the best of you some day."

I don't bother to deny it. Dad's right.

In part. My temper wasn't the only reason I lost it on Kai. My fears about relationships and being left behind reared their ugly head and I pushed Kai away before he could leave me.

I thought I was over this. I thought I'd dealt with my fears.

I thought wrong.

And now I've lost everything.

Chapter 34

"Plot Twist: Taylor Swift has entered the chat."
~ Kai

KAI

"I don't want to go out tonight," I whine.

Jaxon grunts. "If I have to go, you do too."

Blossom elbows him. "Come on, nerd boy. It'll be fun."

He frowns. "Your definition of fun is incorrect."

"I don't care if you don't want to go out," Dakota declares. "We have a babysitter and we're going out. This discussion is over."

Rhett drops an arm over her shoulders and kisses her hair. "There you go, causing havoc again, Havoc."

She rolls her eyes at him.

"How about I babysit little Stephanie? It'll give Eli and Paisley the chance to go out."

Miles shackles my wrist before I can escape. "Nice try. But Eli isn't ready to leave his baby girl alone with anyone."

"I'm not anyone. I'm Uncle Kai. Everyone's favorite uncle."

"You also gave Stephanie a fake ID."

I shrug. "You can never start too early."

"She isn't ready for sippy cups yet. Let alone a fake ID."

"Whatever. Can you release me now?" I tug my arm but he doesn't let me go.

"No. We're going out. It's a Raider family event. You have to go."

I scan the group on my doorstep and relief fills me when I realize I have an ace in the hole. "Zane's not here."

Eli is excused because Paisley just had their baby, but Zane has to attend for tonight to be considered a family event.

"He's meeting us at the bar."

Shit. There's only one way to get out of this.

"I can't go anywhere. I have explosive diarrhea."

"No worries. I have extra diapers from Mira in my bag." Dakota digs through her bag and pulls out a diaper.

Rhett chuckles. "It might be a bit small."

"Does it matter when he's obviously lying?" Jaxon asks.

I growl. "I'm not lying."

"Sure, you are. You always use the explosive diarrhea excuse. You claimed you had diarrhea so often when you were skipping classes in high school, the principal called the house. She was ready to send an ambulance."

"It's true." Rhett nods. "You're lucky I answered the phone instead of Mom."

I glare at them. "I hate all of you."

"Not me," Blossom declares. "I'm a bundle of delight."

"Whatever. Let's go."

I make my way toward my SUV but Miles grabs my wrist again and drags me toward Rhett's vehicle. "You're not driving."

"I can drive. I'm not planning to drink." Because there's no way I can drink away my sorrows with my family and not admit Harper dumped me without a second thought.

My chest squeezes and I nearly stumble. I can't believe she wouldn't let me explain. Granted, I fucked up. I should have been there for her.

But can't I make one mistake? I've proven to her over and over again how I've grown up. How serious I am about her. How much I love her.

I rub my chest as pain blossoms. I freaking love her and she kicked me to the curb over one measly mistake.

Okay. Fine. It was more than one measly mistake. But I could hardly tell her I was building the ramp in advance. It would have ruined the surprise.

Except I was the one who ended up surprised.

"Where are we going?" I ask once Rhett is driving.

"You'll see," Blossom sings.

"I still say we should blindfold him," Miles says.

"There's no reason to blindfold me. I'm here, aren't I?" Under protest, but I'm here.

I study everyone's faces but no one will meet my gaze. Crap on a retired smuggler. They're up to something. And when the Raiders are up to something, the world holds its breath.

Rhett parks in downtown Smuggler's Rest and we pile out of the vehicle. I aim for *Smuggler's Cove* but Miles catches me and shoves me in the other direction.

"I don't want to go to *Bootlegger*," I whine.

Mermaid Karaoke season might be over but the bar remains a pick-up joint. I have no interest in picking up anyone. Unless her name is Harper and she's the grumpiest, stubbornest bar owner on the island.

"Good thing we're not going to *Bootlegger* then," Miles says and steers me into an alleyway.

I plant my feet. "No way. No how."

"Come on," he cajoles. "*Rumrunner* has the best dart boards."

"We should alert the emergency room if Dakota is playing darts," Blossom says.

Dakota glares at her. "I am not playing darts."

"Phew. There aren't enough bandages in the bar if you decide to play."

"Let's get burgers at the *Salty Siren* instead. Since Dakota doesn't want to go to the *Rumrunner* either."

Dakota grins up at me before threading her arm through mine. "I want to go to *Rumrunner*."

I narrow my eyes at her. "You just lost one free babysitter."

"Please, as if you can resist Mira and Pearl."

"I'm serious, Dakota. This is cruel. I never thought you were a cruel woman."

Rhett growls. "Dakota isn't cruel. Watch your language."

Dakota pats my arm. "It'll be okay."

"No, it won't. I did everything right with Harper – treated her well, spoiled her with little gifts, paid attention to her, was there for her, acted nothing like my dad – and she left me anyway."

Rhett whirls around to face me. "Hold on. Nothing like Dad? Are you worried you're going to turn into him?"

"Mom says I'm the spitting image of him."

"Having the same appearance as him, doesn't make you him."

I drop my chin and study the ground before I admit, "But I'm a goofball. I don't take work seriously. Dad was the same."

"You're also twenty-four. Give yourself a break."

I growl. I've had enough of being reminded of my age. It's just a number.

"This is my fault," Jaxon says and I whip my head up to meet his gaze.

"Your fault?"

"I shouldn't have been so hard on you."

"No, you were right. I was goofing off at work and you were handling my responsibilities."

"Not anymore, I'm not."

My brow wrinkles. "What?"

He clears his throat. "Ever since we had our conversation, you've changed. You show up at work on time. You get your tasks done. You've proven to me you can be the operations manager of the distillery. I should have told you as much."

"See? You are nothing like Dad," Miles says. "You would never abandon one of us when we need you. Even when we drag you to Mermaid Karaoke when all you want to do is spend time with Harper."

I scan the faces of my brothers and Dakota and Blossom. All of them are nodding in agreement.

Are they right? Can I believe them? I blow out a breath.

"Okay. I'm not Dad." I hope. "But Harper did leave me."

Blossom threads her arm through mine. "Let's go get her back."

Hope ignites in my belly. "Do you think I have a chance?"

"Let's go find out."

I allow her to lead me to the speakeasy door. The bouncer, Trent, opens it before anyone has a chance to knock. I'm doing this. I'm going to fight for the woman I love.

Dakota shoves me inside and the music starts up. I groan when I realize the song is *We Are Never Getting Back Together*. Awesome. Taylor Swift is on Harper's side.

Hold on. This isn't Taylor Swift singing. My eyes nearly bug out of my head when I realize it's Harper on the stage, belting out the lyrics.

So much for having a chance. Harper's message is loud and clear. We are never getting back together.

I whirl around – intent on escaping – but Jaxon stops me. "Trust me. You don't want to leave."

"Trust me. I do."

I struggle to escape his hold, but he's not letting me go. In fact, he's pushing me closer and closer to the stage. And now Harper is singing directly to me.

Except she's no longer singing about how we'll never get back together. She's singing about Christmas lights and our house and making our own rules.

My heart gets stuck in my throat as I listen to her sing *Lover*. She smiles down at me. It's one of her dazzling smiles with her dimples fully on display.

The song finishes and the place erupts in cheers.

"What does everyone think?" she asks the crowd. "Should we never get back together?"

My heart forgets how to beat as I wait for the crowd's reaction. Everyone boos. Especially my family.

"Or should I reinstate Kai as my lover?"

The crowd breaks into a chant. "Lover. Lover. Lover."

I don't need any more encouragement. This is my chance and I'm grabbing it with both hands. Harper is not getting rid of me.

I jump on the stage. I snatch the microphone from her and drop it on the floor.

"Were you pranking me?"

"It depends. Did you fall for it?"

"My heart broke into a million pieces as I listened to you sing."

She pats my chest and I dare to wrap my arms around her. When she doesn't protest, I draw her closer.

"I'm sorry about your heart, but I think I won the prank war for you."

"I don't give a shit about the prank war. Although I am very proud of you for letting loose and letting your goofy show."

She bites her bottom lip and looks up at me from beneath her lashes. "You're my goofy."

My heart makes a gallant effort to beat its way out of my chest. "I am?"

"If you want to be."

"Slugger, I want to be your everything."

"Why didn't you tell me about the ramp?"

"I wanted to surprise you. I wanted to give you something you and your dad need. It wasn't about showing off."

She palms my face and I close my eyes as peace washes over me. I never thought I'd feel her skin against mine again. "Thank you," she whispers before her lips meet mine.

I moan before slipping my tongue into her mouth. Her taste of beer and vanilla hits me. Home. This is home. This is where I belong. In Harper's arms.

"Get a room!" Miles shouts, and I wrench my lips from Harper's.

The entire bar is full of people watching us. Dakota and Blossom clap and whoop while Rhett and Jaxon nod in approval. Meanwhile, Miles is on his way to the bar already.

"I love you, Harper Poole. I am never letting you go."

She needs to know what she signed up for when she took this stage and accepted me.

"I love you, Kai Raider. I am never letting you go, either. Although, I did buy you a power bank for your phone."

I bark out a laugh. "Of course, you did."

"Dad says hi. He also says I have a temper and you need to tame it."

My blood heats. "Tame it? No one can tame my slugger." But I'm going to do my best.

She wiggles and my cock – hard and heavy – presses against her. "Let's go handle your little problem."

"Why, Harper Poole? Are you suggesting a secret rendezvous in the storage room?"

She snorts. "No way. I have an office. It has a couch. And it locks with a key."

"Let's go." I lead her to the edge of the stage and jump off. Once I'm on the ground, I grasp her hips and help her down. She wraps her legs around my waist. "Good girl," I mutter as I begin to carry her to the back.

A baby cries in the background and Harper pauses. "Rhett and Dakota brought Mira?"

My brow wrinkles. "No. They didn't."

I glance over her shoulder. My jaw drops open when I locate the source of the sound. Zane is standing near the bar holding a baby in his arms. What the hell is going on?

Chapter 35

"This is definitely not the delivery I was expecting."
~ Zane

Zane

The doorbell rings and I rush toward it.

"I'm coming. Hold your smugglers!"

I fling the door open and smile at Miles. Except it's not Miles on my doorstep. It's a beautiful woman. I dial up the smile and flash her my dimples.

"Why, hello."

She rolls her eyes. "You don't remember me, do you?"

I rake my gaze over her body. "Maybe I need a refresher."

Forget about going to *Rumrunner* to watch Harper humiliate Kai. I prefer a warm, naked body in my bed. I open the door and motion her inside.

"Do you want to come in?"

"No, but she will."

She will? My brow furrows. There's no one else on my porch.

"She? Who?"

She reaches down to pick up her bag. No, this isn't a bag. This is a baby car seat. And it isn't empty. There's an actual baby sleeping in it. The woman tries to hand the car seat to me but I fling my hands in the air and back up.

I have no idea what's going on but I am not accepting a baby from a virtual stranger. Let's face it. I'm not accepting a baby from anyone other than my brothers or their wives. Other babies? No way. No how.

"What exactly is going on here?"

"I didn't realize you were this slow. You certainly weren't slow in bed."

I scowl. I can be slow in bed. I prefer not to. Fast and furious is way more fun in my opinion. But how does she know about my preferences in bed?

"Have we met before?"

She sighs. "It's a good thing you're pretty because smart you are not."

"I'm not stupid."

"Let me give you a refresher. Yes, we've met before. Yes, this is your baby. And bye-bye."

She sets the baby car seat back on the ground and whirls around to escape. I catch her wrist before she can flee.

"What the hell? You can't leave me a baby. I don't even know your name."

She spits daggers out of her eyes at me. "Do you sleep with so many women, you can't remember all of their names?"

Technically, I never sleep with women. I undress them, give them an orgasm or two, and then I leave. Sleeping isn't involved.

I scratch my neck. "I suck at remembering names."

"Could you be any lamer?"

I'm starting to get annoyed. I didn't make this woman any promises. I never do. I'm always clear. A night of fun with no strings attached. Nothing else is on offer. And it never will be.

"I'm sorry, I don't remember you." It's not a lie. "Why don't you come in and we can discuss this?"

"There's nothing to discuss. Adele is your baby. I'm done raising her on my own. You're up."

"How do I know this...," I manage to stop myself before I say a thing. "Adele is mine?"

She plants a fist on her hip. "Are you saying I'm a slut?"

"How the hell would I know if you're a slut? I don't know who you are!"

"Don't you dare yell at me in front of the baby," she hisses.

I inhale a deep breath. I'm not one to yell at people. Especially not a woman I don't know. Or, at least, don't remember. I'm usually laid back, but this situation is not usual.

"Let's start over. I'm Zane and you are?"

I hold out my hand and she stares at it for a few long moments before finally placing her hand in mine.

"Daisy."

I flash her a smile. "Hi, Daisy. It's lovely to see you again."

"I wish I could say the same," she mutters.

I nod to the baby. "And this little girl is yours?"

"Ours. She's ours."

I grit my teeth before I lash out. I might enjoy playing in the sheets with women but I'm always careful. Always. Babies are not on my agenda. I have no interest in becoming a parent.

"I always use protection. You're certain Adele is mine?"

"I'm certain and now I'm done with this conversation."

She whirls around to leave again and panic strikes. She can't leave this tiny creature behind. I have no idea how to handle a baby.

"You can't abandon your baby with me."

"She's your baby, too."

Okay. Fine. "You can't abandon our baby with me."

"You're up. I'm done being a single mom. I'm done missing out on all the fun. I'm done with missing classes."

Classes? She must be a college student. I file the information away for future use.

"I'm sorry you're having a difficult time. Let's discuss this. Let's figure out a solution."

"I have the solution. Daddy's going to raise Adele. Discussion over."

She sprints to her car. I start to chase after her but the baby screams. I stare at her for a second before I swear and reach down to pick her up.

"Shush, baby. Don't cry."

I rock her in my arms and she immediately settles. Phew.

"What am I going to do with you?" She stares up at me with big blue eyes. The same blue eyes I gaze into every morning in the mirror.

Shit. Is this baby mine? What am I going to do?

I do the same thing I've always done when I need help. I go in search of my brothers.

Chapter 36

"Nothing says romance like acoustic insulation." ~ Harper

HARPER

"Dad!" I shout as I shut the front door behind me. "I'm home."

I frown when I notice his usual spot in front of the television is empty. Granted, he doesn't spend as much time binge watching crime shows since the cast is off of his arm and he's able to get around on his own again. But still. Where could he be?

I set the bag of groceries in the kitchen before continuing my search. Dad better not be mowing the lawn. There's no reason to exert his independence since Kai is now doing all of the mowing.

"Dad!" I shout again as I make my way down the hallway toward his bedroom.

I stop when I notice the door to my bedroom is closed. Why is it closed? I always keep my bedroom door open during the day.

I peek my head inside my room. "Hello?"

Dad claps. "Hot damn! It works!"

Dad and Kai are sitting in the little sitting area – because apparently I need a sitting area in my bedroom to read my romance novels at – near the window.

"What's going on? And do I want to know?"

Kai jumps to his feet and bounds toward me. He plants a quick kiss on my lips before wrapping his arms around my waist and throwing me in the air. "It worked!"

"What worked?"

"The soundproofing."

Soundproofing? I push on his shoulders until he sets me down. "Back up. Start from the beginning."

"I soundproofed the room. This way you won't be bothered by Henry's snoring at night anymore."

"Sounds like heaven."

"And to prevent Henry from hearing us." He waggles his eyebrows in case I'm confused as to what noises Dad would overhear.

"There's my cue to exit," Dad grumbles as he pushes to his feet. Kai rushes to help him but Dad bats his hands away. "I can stand on my own."

Kai retreats but he trails behind Dad as he leaves. Those two have formed a special bond. I'm glad. Kai deserves to have a dad who won't abandon him. Abandoning people isn't part of the Poole family genes.

Once Dad is safely in the living room, Kai returns to me. "Hi, Slugger. How was the grocery store? Did you beat up any women?"

I scowl at him. "I've never beat up any women at a grocery store."

He wraps his arms around me and kisses my forehead. "Sure, you haven't."

"Thanks for doing the soundproofing. It's going to come in handy for me next summer."

"I think you mean for us."

I roll my eyes. "Fine. Us. If I let you sleep over."

"You can't sleep over in your own house."

"You can't… what?"

"I think it's about time we made this thing official and moved in together."

"I can't leave Dad."

"Which is why I soundproofed your room."

I clear my throat. "Let me get this straight. You've decided to move in? We're not going to discuss this?"

"Nope." He kisses my nose.

"Nice try. We're discussing this."

He leans his forehead against mine. "What is there to discuss? I love you. You love me. We should live together."

"This is a big step."

"Do you want to hear the elevator pitch?"

I widen my eyes. Kai never ceases to surprise and amaze me. I imagine I'll be ninety years old and wearing adult diapers and he'll surprise me. "Do you have a pitch prepared?"

"It's possible I knew my grumpy woman wouldn't accept me moving in without making a fuss."

"Okay. Let's hear it."

He hesitates. "I don't have a computer for my PowerPoint presentation."

"Kai Raider, you did not prepare a PowerPoint presentation and I know it."

"Fine." He huffs. "Here are the advantages to me moving in. One, you have someone to help with Henry. Two, I look hot mowing the lawn without my shirt on. Three, you'll have orgasms on tap. And, four, I'll help with the rent."

"I don't pay rent."

"Excuse me. I misspoke. I'll help pay the mortgage."

I bristle. "I don't need your help to pay the mortgage."

"Nevertheless, if I'm living here, I need to contribute to the costs."

"It's unnecessary. I don't like this."

He squeezes my hands. "I do. It means your monthly household costs are lower."

Which means I can increase my loan payments for *Bootlegger*, thereby paying off the loan quicker and getting out of debt faster. I never should have told him about my financial struggles with the bar.

"I don't need you to save me."

"Good. Because I'm not saving you. I'm helping you. And your dad, of course."

I narrow my eyes at him. "Be honest. Are you moving in because of me or my dad?"

He grins. "You said moving in. You're giving in."

I don't deny it since he's right. "What chance do I have against your charm?"

He smirks. "None. Because you love me."

"You're a pain in my ass."

His eyes sparkle. "I can be a pain in your ass if you want."

I shove him. "You keep away from my ass."

"But it's so delightful to bite."

"You're annoying."

"You're confusing annoying with delightful."

"No, I'm really not."

He winds an arm around my waist and draws me near. "Are we doing this, Slugger? Am I moving in?"

I scrunch my nose and pretend to consider the matter. There's nothing to consider. Of course, he's moving in. I want Kai with me every night. I want to sleep in his arms and wake up with him every morning.

"Do you need me to convince you?" He presses his hard length into my stomach and I gasp.

"How are you hard now? We're in the middle of a serious conversation."

He shrugs. "I can't help it. The sexiest woman in the universe is in my arms. Naturally, I'm excited." He nips my chin. "The question is. What are you going to do about it?"

"I don't know. I need to put the groceries away. I have to work in an hour. I probably should cook dinner for Dad before I leave."

"You should probably kiss me and let me thank you for letting me move in."

And how are you going to thank me?"

"With lots and lots of orgasms."

"Dang. I can't argue with your logic. It's pretty sound."

He grins and his blue eyes sparkle with pleasure. "You're sure? You want me to move in?"

"The first time you leave the toilet seat up, you're sleeping on the sofa."

"Toilet seat down. Got it."

"And you're in charge of dinner on nights I work."

"I'll be in charge of cooking whenever you want. Anything to keep you from cooking. Do we have a deal?"

I nod.

"Let's seal it with a kiss."

I push up on my toes but before his mouth can meet mine, Dad shouts, "Are you two done yet? I'm hungry."

Kai barks out a laugh, and I bury my face in his chest. "Are you sure this is the life you want?"

He pinches my chin. "Hell yeah, it is. It's the life I've always dreamed of."

"Smooth talker."

"Smooth talker who loves you."

Those words hit me in the chest before spreading warmth throughout my body. I hope they always do.

"I love you, too."

"Now, let's go feed your dad before he calls the fire department."

"This is why he's not allowed a cell phone."

Kai grasps my hand and leads me toward the hallway. "Thank goodness you couldn't resist my sexy ass."

He saunters toward the kitchen before I have a chance to respond. But I do watch his sexy ass as he struts away. He's right. I didn't have a chance to resist him and I wouldn't want it any other way.

About the Author

D.E. Haggerty is an American who has spent the majority of her adult life abroad. She has lived in Istanbul, various places throughout Germany, and currently finds herself in The Hague. She has been a military policewoman, a lawyer, a B&B owner/operator and now a writer.

Manufactured by Amazon.ca
Bolton, ON